I AM THE CHILDREN I TEACH

TONYA BLUE

Published By

Blue Purse Publishing
P.O. Box 22698
Baltimore, MD 21203
http://www.TonyaBlue.com

Copyright © 2010 by Tonya Blue

All rights reserved. No part of this book may be reproduced or transmitted in any form or by any means, including electronic, written, or mechanical, digital, including photocopying and recording, or by any information storage or retrieval system except as may be expressly permitted in writing by the author.

* This book contains mature content. Parents should read the book and determine its appropriateness for use with their children.

First paperback edition October 2010

Cover Design: Steven Kreichauf
Editor: *Various Marks*

Manufactured in the United States of America

ISBN 978-0-9830071-0-4

This book is dedicated to the most important people in my life—

Mom, Dad, Danny, Grandma, Jazz, and Angie.

ACKNOWLEDGEMENTS

God's timing is always perfect and for that I thank Him. This book was written for His glory, for I am His maidservant working to help free others from the stronghold of pain.

To my mom, Ella Blue, the woman who introduced me to God's love at a young age. Where would I be without you or God? I am a better woman because of the example you are everyday. I hope I have made you proud. Thank you for being my mom, friend, prayer warrior, confidant, and example of what a woman of God should be. I love you.

To my dad, Eddie S. Blue, the only man who calls me Renea and the only man I will ever answer to. You give me strength and courage when I'm not sure I have it. I am you in my classroom—strict, no nonsense, confidant, yet fair. I know Nana is looking down on us both smiling. She is proud of you just like I am. Thank you for giving me the best parts of you. I love you, Daddy.

To Danny E. Blue, my big brother & biggest fan, I never knew I had my own cheering squad until I looked in your direction and there you were. Your prayers over the telephone, pictures through the mail, and my Skype camera to keep me connected with the family helped more than you know. You have showed me it's never too late, even when others discourage you. For this, I am forever grateful and humble. I love you, your kid sister.

Eddie E. Blue, my brother, we may not get along, but we have some much in common. Like you and Uncle Buddy, I am a writer, too. I hope this commonality brings us closer. Love ya!

My angels, Cynthia (C.M.), Keshawn (the true hustler), & Sonja (the stylist extraordinaire), my sisters my friends. I thank God for bringing me my three sisters, when I had none. Your support and love for me and my dream cannot be expressed through words. We have lived, laughed, loved, eaten, cried, prayed, fasted, shared success, and loss. What more could a woman ask for, except more time with you? Thank you for being there for me during every step of this process. See you on the plane to O.

Jessica, Natasha, Joanne, Natale, & Michelle, the people you work with make working so much fun. Thank you for reading, going to book fairs, handing out bookmarks and postcards, and for just being there for me when I was nervous, tired, and unsure of myself. Your brainstorming power was a great gift, but your friendship is the best.

Steve Kreichauf, the book cover is amazing. Thank you for your hard work and dedication to this project and for believing in my vision.

Keisha Crowell & Joy Campbell, the first readers of my manuscript 5 years ago.

Thanks for reading an unfinished manuscript and seeing what it could really become.

Bishop, Lady D, & the Kingdom Worship Center family, where I am trained, equipped, empowered, and mobilized. I am grateful to be under such a covering. In this season of Re- I have been restored, revived, and renewed. Thank you Bishop, my spiritual father. Love you.

Pastor Greg & Pastor Tonya, thank you for your prayers, excitement, and believing in me. I am grateful and blessed to have you as a part of my life. Your guidance has helped me to move through this process with ease. I have named my process and it is called Victory for I am a conqueror.

Southwest Academy/Dunbar Middle School/Harlem Park Middle School families, thank you for giving me my stripes, teaching legs, and the opportunity to learn and grow. Thank you for being my family.

The brothers, from another mother Curtis, Jahmal, Scott, Sherin, Groleua, and Queen, thank you for looking out for me even when you didn't know it and encouraging me in this process.

To my sista-girls, Jeanne, Annette, Dani, Karisma, Melissa, Shanette, Eboni, Lore, Nikki, Kim, Sharita, Rochelle, Silean, Naelis, Barron, Elisha, Tulip, "MA", Pastor Vikki, Tracy, Yolanda, Sonya W., Karma, Z, and Jamie, thank you for being you and supporting me.

To all the families, who have supported me: The Blue family, The Clark family, The Pugh family, The Cummings Family, The Schloss family, The Green family, The Shirley family, The Wilson family, The Golson family, The Johnson family, The Phillips family, The Rogers family, The Jackson family, The Barnes family, The Richard family, The Jefferson family, The Skinner family, The Williams family, The Evans family, and The Walley family.

To Various Marks & VeRonda, you are the absolute best. I was blessed when you became a part of my life professionally and now personally. I couldn't have asked for a better editor or friend. Let's get started on the next book.

To my students, over the past 12 years, thank you. I have learned you can't reach everybody, but if you can reach just one… your work is not in vain. I now know this to be true. Seeing you in college, working, raising families, and realizing that there is a world out there waiting for you does my heart glad. Thank you for allowing me to be a part of your lives. We had some bumps, bruises, and a lot of growing up to do, but we made it. I pray that the impact that we have had on each other's lives makes us better people every day. I know my life will never be the same. I am better because of you.

PREFACE

MS. BROWN

I never wanted to be a teacher. I did not like kids and for that reason, I was not a mother. If a pregnancy scare occurred or if the man I was dating said something about meeting his kid(s), my immediate thought process was to, 'make an appointment at the clinic or I am not their mother, why do they need to meet me?' I did not like kids.

How I became a teacher I will never know. When I listen to my colleagues talk about how they wanted to be teachers since they were 5 years old —I laugh. I don't remember what I used to tell people I wanted to be, but I knew for sure it wasn't a teacher. I never had the patience or the desire to understand any child's behavior or lack thereof. What problems could a 12- to 15-year-old child possibly face that would merit the disrespect they shoved upon adults? None, as far as I was concerned. Children go to school, complete household chores, and play video games. Children have no true responsibilities like bills, relationships, or real health problems. Yeah, kids are overweight because they don't exercise; disrespectful because there is no discipline in the home; and lazy because they have no work ethic. Right? At least this is what I thought. For a long time, I carried these perceptions with me, for the majority of my teaching career.

To me, teaching children is very similar to having a relationship with a man. Some children, like men, are great during the honeymoon stage; you know the first 3 months... More like the first 3 minutes—Ha! They make me smile because they are everything I hoped for and they work hard at the relationship. Both men and children give attention, time, and affection, but it varies in how it is given. Students complete assignments, are well behaved, and respectful. Men call, take me out, and finesse me with words of the future and then BAM—the truth. The true habits and true personalities come out and I am disappointed. The façade is over. For students, assignments are no longer handed in. They are now cursing me out and in constant conflict over who the adult is in the room. The once studious behavior is now gone and my grade book looks like someone shot holes in it from all of the zeros it displays. The man no longer calls, his quality time with me is rare, he is inconsiderate, and sexual intimacy has become his number one priority. As a teacher and a woman I am angry and frustrated because I thought the relationship was working. I was giving my all—and for what? Disappointment! A mutual relationship, not hardly. I guess I can't have a mutual relationship with some students, or some men either, for that matter.

This is where the relationship between men and children differ. I can leave the man if he continues to disappoint me, but I am stuck with my students for another 7 months and the abuse continues. Perceptions begin to change and then the relationship becomes unhealthy because my heart has been broken. No matter how many times I may say to myself, meet them where they are and not where I am, disappointment begins my day and my expectations are lowered... Talk about an abusive relationship. The once strong belief I had for a successful relationship is now bleak and I am just going through the motions to make it to the end of the school year.

What happened to the relationship that was being built? Maybe it never was. Maybe it was all in my mind. I am alone again in a relationship even though there are 32 other people in the room with me. When I stand in front of my classroom ready to begin instruction and hear, "that bitch thinks she's cute," I don't see children. I hadn't been in the classroom for 5 minutes and I am already a bitch. And I am supposed to look past that and care about their issues? I don't see them as children. I see the faces of every man or woman who has ever hurt me in the past and I get pissed off! I am standing in front of "children"; girls who are 12 to 15 years old in the eighth grade with big breast, butts, and hips bigger than mine, who are in competition with me for attention. I stand in front of boys who are 12 to 16 years old with facial hair, deep voices, and hungry, hungry appetites for sex already like every other man in the club, lounge, or—yes—even *church*. These same young boys are wondering if they were 10 years older would I go out on a date with them. Hell no!

Similac, television, and the internet have nurtured and raised many of my students and these are some of the children I teach. I never wanted to be a teacher, but I am here now… Have been for 11 years and sometimes I still wonder why? I don't wonder why I am a teacher, but rather, what is truly behind the blank stares on their faces. What thoughts are floating around in their little minds that make them behave in such a manner? For most of my teaching career, I didn't want or care to know, but after meeting two particular students, I had no choice.

BEFORE READING

Determine the meaning...

CHAPTER ONE

THE BOY

I remember how my hustle started, but can't really explain how it got so out of control. I walked in on Unk and his boys watching a porno in the basement. All of them had a bottle of some sort in their hand, one Hennessey, one Remy, and another with a purple bag… and all of them had their hands in their pants. One guy's eyes were closed while he moaned; the other guy's eyes were glued to the TV with his mouth open. There was a bottle of lotion on the badly scratched wooden coffee table when it hit me—OH SHIT—they are jerking off. I almost said something, but then I started to turn around to get out of there when the man with the purple bag asked, "Yo Lil' Shorty, what up? Why you leavin'?"

My Unk opened his eyes, looked at me and said, "you fuck'n with my buzz. Take ya lil' ass upstairs."

The other dude never opened his eyes. He just began to grunt and shake… guess he was busting a nut.

"Sorry, I'm going back upstairs. Didn't know you all were down here," I said as I turned and ran up the steps.

"Damn, I'm soft," said the man with the purple bag.

That is so nasty; at least that's what I thought. From that day on, I never looked at things the same. The man with the purple bag later became the man who changed my life forever and my name, too.

CHAPTER TWO

MS. BROWN

*W*hen she kissed me on the lips, she would stick her tongue in my mouth. That shocked me at first because I had never been kissed like that before, especially not by a girl. I didn't know what to do so I just stuck my tongue out and let her suck on it. She rubbed and squeezed my butt with one hand while she pulled down my purple Under-Roo panties with the other. We lay down on the floor and I just kept my tongue out. She moaned and rubbed on me while she kissed me. Her spit was filling my mouth and it began to run onto my cheek. I giggled because it felt gross, but was so funny, too. She just said it was okay and licked it off my face. She told me to roll over. I lay down on the floor on my stomach and waited. This had happened a few times over time, but now I knew the routine, and I wanted to do it, too. I wanted to rub my stuff and move on her to feel good, too. I didn't know why I continued to let her do this, but for me it was fun, then. Everybody in my class was doing it either with a boy or a girl at least that is what I heard.

This was my introduction to sex and homosexuality at an early age. The prey would become a predator to others. My sexual roadmap had been laid out by several encounters and would shape my mind and behavior for years. I never knew how it would affect me as an adult, my interactions with men, my self-esteem, and my work with children.

Maybe if someone had noticed me, I would be different. This is why I pay close attention to everyone.

CHAPTER THREE

MS. WILSON

I find joy in teaching. Always have. I have a connection with my students that I can't explain. I share their joys and pains sometimes without speaking a word. Right now, I feel his pain more than any of the other students because I have lived his pain. Something is wrong. He missed school for almost a week and hasn't asked for his makeup work yet. That is not like him. He is such a responsible kid, unlike some of my other students. I know he is absent when his mother isn't doing well or if his brother is missing in action. We have talked about it before and he always came back ready and eager to learn with tenacity. When he was in class today he just stared off into space playing with his pencil. When I called his name and asked him a question, he hunched his shoulders. That was his only response. The look on his face—blank. No anger, no sadness, nothing.

I remember having that blank stare when my mother was ill. My sisters and I were around the same age as he is now when Daddy told us Mom had a brain tumor and it needed to be removed. I was hopeful and believed Daddy when he said she would be alright. I believed God would heal her, the doctors were capable, and Daddy wouldn't lie. So, I went on with life as normal. Normalcy didn't last long because Mom got worse. The doctors told us her cancer had progressed at such a rate that surgery wouldn't help. They told Dad he needed to get things in order because she had about a month, maybe two, to live. My life was never the same after that. I wasn't the same after that, even though I had so much family support. I was blessed. I wonder who does he have? What will happen to him? Who will be there for him? The streets are calling his name… Will he answer?

CHAPTER FOUR

The Red-hair, Freckled-face Girl

Dear Diary,

I woke up wet again. My t-shirt and my underwear was wet, but for different reasons. I have been having the same fuck'n nightmare since I moved to this hell hole. I can still feel the pain and smell his nasty ass breath. I can still see my mother's face and hear her screaming, calling me a bitch, and telling me to get out of her house while she was hugging my brother. I don't know how I feel about anything anymore. I am suppose to start my sessions with that lady, Ms. Betty, this week to talk about the situation. Fuck that! I want to know how long they gonna keep me here. I don't want to talk to nobody about nuttin'. Ain't nobody bidness. Ain't nobody wanna talk to me when they took me out da house, why they wanna talk now?

Shit, I gotta get some sleep 'cause I'm starting to fall asleep in class and I don't need to hear about that shit, either. But every time I go to sleep I hear my mom yelling and see him holding her back, saying something 'bout protecting someone. Who da fuck he gonna protect? She was coming after me like she was really gonna fight me. Her own daughter. She wanna fuck me up! I still can't believe she put me out. She didn't listen to a word I had to say. I kept trying to tell her, but she kept yelling and yelling and yelling! She only listened to him, that fuck'n ass hole. She hates me. I hate me, but I hate him and this fuck'n place more.

DURING READING

Make connections…

CHAPTER FIVE

Ms. Wilson

A simple assignment, opened a door I wish I could lock shut. I asked my class to share their journal entry about overcoming a challenge and to explain how they overcame it. What a mistake that was. I try to have students connect real life situations to the skills we learn in class and it usually works, but today was different. I am not saying it didn't work, I just found out too much information. Today's sharing was just too insightful.

Ms. Brown, "Brownie" to those closest to her, is my best girlfriend and colleague. She teaches eighth-grade Reading down the hall from me. Brownie is tall, light skinned, with sandy brown hair, and freckles on her nose and cheeks, with the most intimidating brown eyes I have ever seen. As soft as they are, she uses those eyes to keep her students in check. I was intrigued by the writing prompts strategy she used during instruction and decided to use it during my instruction today. She has been doing things like this for as long as we have been friends, 9 years, and it still works. She even takes it a step further using music and modern day lyrics for examples to help her students learn and to keep them engaged; I am more old fashioned.

Engagement for both of us as educators is key and this is our strongest similarity, as discipline is never a problem for us like it is for some of our other colleagues (especially some of the Caucasian teachers). Some teachers want to be the student's friend at the same time. That doesn't work? Parents can't be parents and friends; although they try and seem to fail, as far as the results I see demonstrated. Conversely, educators can't be too friendly and maintain control of 30 kids at the same time. Kids need structure and they yearn for it even when they don't know they want it. A true educator can't teach without it. Brownie and I both believe that, but I am a little more understanding than Brownie. She is thick skinned with a venomous tongue, full of wit and satire. She takes no prisoners, children, and colleagues alike. "No excuses" is her mantra. Me, I understand situations and leave room for second chances.

Brownie doesn't like to give students too many chances. She thinks they will begin to take advantage of the situation. This is as true as there are kids, but if we don't give them a second chance than who will? My daddy always told me everybody deserves a second chance and I agree, especially with our students. Brownie doesn't agree with me. She isn't really too fond of disrespectful children. I believe disrespectful children are crying out for help, attention, love, and guidance. Boy, do we differ here.

Anyway, I wonder what she would have thought of my lesson today when the kids shared the challenged they faced and how they overcame them. Talk about life giving you a second chance. For all her hardness she would have probably done the same thing I did, stood there with her mouth wide open. What some of my kids' face I would have difficulty handling as an adult, not to mention at their age. Times have truly changed. The issues they face are more intense and dictate if they will survive in this world. Survival of the fittest has a different meaning now. One of my girls shared that she had been arrested six times and she was now trying to change her life. For the most part, my other students listened as if this revelation was an insignificant happenstance. She went on to explain that she didn't want to go to "baby bookings", the juvenile detention center, anymore for selling weed and "other stuff." She said she wanted to find a better way, a legal way to help her mom. What is wrong with her mom?

I couldn't believe it. She just told us that she had been arrested for selling drugs and had gone to jail? I am still shocked and so were some of my kids. My classroom went grave silent. This girl just didn't get a second chance... she got a third, fourth, fifth, and sixth chance. I told Brownie you never know what is going on with the kids once they leave our classroom or the school. You just hope that they come back the next day, a little better than before. Wait until I tell Calvin about this.

CHAPTER SIX

The Red-hair, Freckled-face Girl

Dear Diary,

Today in class Ms. Brown got on my nerves. She don't get it. Did she even hear me when I told her I was in time out? She just like the rest of them, she don't listen. Do she have any idea what it's like to be in time out in a hell hole like this? She was going on and on about her stupid ass homework. That bitch think she cute. She must think I give a dayum about her calling the home telling them I don't do her stupid homework. These fuck'n people ain't my parents! I didn't even wanna go to school today anyway. I couldn't sleep. It's dark and cold in that room. It shouldn't be called time out. More like fuck'n jail! Lock down!... Something. I always have nightmares after I have been in time out. But, does Ms. Brown care about that? NO! She just cares about her stupid ass homework. Fuck her and her homework! I would cuss her out but instead I just stare in that ugly, freckled face of hers. She's black. How did she get them anyway? I know that pisses her off, fuck'n bitch. She can't threaten me with that "I'ma call ya momma" shit because I don't even live with my momma. My momma ain't coming up here to whoop my ass in front of da class like dat other girl momma did last month. She don't even want me in the house. I still can't believe she let them take me away and my brother gets to stay with him. I wish I was back home with my mother. Things would be different. I wouldn't be living in no stupid group home and I wouldn't be in no dumb ass time out room either. They won't let me go home because of what I did, but what about what he did to me? He still lives there and I can't. Shit ain't fair!

CHAPTER SEVEN

THE BOY

Today Ms. Wilson's class was crazy. We discussed our challenging experiences and how we got over them. This one girl told us about how she had gone to jail. Ms. Wilson was standing in her usual place in front of the room at her podium looking crazy. She was shocked, we weren't. Most of us had heard about it already so we didn't say anything. The girl had moved into the neighborhood a few blocks from me about 4 weeks ago and was already working for Mike Mike. I don't know how she did that. Mike don't trust nobody especially somebody new. He is the biggest, blackest, scariest looking dude I ever saw, but he keeps his braids tight. He don't play when it come to his money. Maybe he knew her before or he liked her because she acted just like a dude on the street. I don't know, but I am sure he wouldn't want her talking about her selling in class. I wonder if she knows my brother?

After she read her entry, no one wanted to read. Ms. Wilson asked for volunteers and nobody moved. I looked at Ms. Wilson and raised my hand. She smiled like she was relieved. I did it because Ms. Wilson is cool. I would do anything for her. Ms. Wilson has long dreads that she wears in a ponytail and she wears square glasses with her big cheeks. She looks like my mommy before she got sick and she is nice like her, too. So I read mine about how my mom was sick and that sometimes it is hard to focus on school work. I told them that I get over my challenge by reading books, writing my Unk, and talking with my brother. My brother takes care of us. When I said Unk, Ms. Wilson made a face so I changed it to my Uncle. Ms. Wilson nodded and smiled. She always told us to use our "paycheck" vocabulary (speak proper English). She told us we will not get the careers we want speaking slang. Ms Brown, my Reading teacher, tells us that, too.

One boy, the "Boy with the Mohawk" said something smart about me reading. I couldn't really hear him. I really didn't care. I liked reading. It kept my mind off what was going on with my mommy, our living situation, and the fact that there wasn't much I could do about it. I hated seeing her like that, but what could I do? Just deal with it, I guess.

CHAPTER EIGHT

MS. BROWN

Umph, children burn me up. It's a shame how a child can change my demeanor or my entire day with their presence alone. The future delinquents in training! I tried Wilson's, "Willie" for short, "room for a second chance" idea and it gets me nothing, but mad. Willie can deal with that mess because she believes it. She is old fashioned and animated with her teaching style, and her interaction with students. She likes to tell stories and entertain her students with her colorful personality. Willie's a cocoa colored, full-figured sista with beautiful long dreads. Her plump face seems to always have a permanent smile as she glides through her room with her full hips and high heels. How she wears high heels to work every day on these concrete floors is beyond me. Oh yeah, she claps her hands, jumps around making facial expressions, and tells "nickelodeon-type" stories. She is such a softie. Me, huh, I tell it like it is. No room to sugar coat the truth… Take your feelings to someone who cares. Do what I say and keep it moving—you suspects.

The little red-hair, freckled-face girl ticked me off today. She sits there and doesn't participate, doesn't complete assignments, and ignores me when I ask her questions. I use to think she was just one of the quiet ones, cute, because she had freckles like me. Not anymore. She is just disrespectful like the rest of them. Willie said I sound like a kid having a tantrum. I know. So what—I'm mad! Willie says remember that kids have bad days, too. Whatever! A bad day for a kid is the video game didn't work last night. BAD DAY MY ASS!

Oh, not to mention in the middle of instruction another kid has his cell phone under the desk texting someone. When I took the phone from him, he had a fit. Telling me how he was texting his mother and he needs his phone back or he will get in trouble. He didn't complete the assignment to compose a paragraph, but he can compose a text message. This is too much. The kids were enjoying the lesson and working when these two students changed the entire classroom climate. I know I should keep going and hand him one of those b/s slips that says see me after class, but sometimes it's hard for me to let go of the negative stuff. I have been doing it for years, remembering negative experiences and situations, and using them as land marks for memories and a guide on how to live my life.

I know one thing for sure, those two won't get second chances when it comes to adding in participation points when its report card time… Unlike the girl Willie told me about who received more than a second chance from the state. Children are something else. Either they are disrespectful or living an adult life. What does Ms. Woodrow call it?... a "parentified child." Children who act like the parents at home and bring that persona to our classrooms. Yeah, I got your "parentified child" when I knock you out. I am the only adult in C-2. The girl was arrested six times for taking care of her mom—illegally. Really?... Selling drugs to take care of her trifling behind momma. Who was taking care of her? I tell you, I may be intimidating, and mean to some of these anti-social students, but I am a protector. If life has taught me nothing else, it has taught me to protect the weak.

CHAPTER NINE

MS. WILSON

I love my baby, Calvin, but I hate it when he's right because he gloats forever. Calvin is 6-foot 4 and huge. I mean John Coffee, from the Green Mile, huge. Bald head, hazel eyes, and a goatee to frame the lips I love to kiss. He is too big to physically gloat around our two-bedroom apartment when he is right. Our apartment is cozy enough for us and his two kids when they come over during the week and on weekends. Modest size living room, and dining area, but our kitchen is small. The tan colored cabinets, stove, and refrigerator are all on the same wall, leaving little space for Calvin and I to maneuver around with ease. I don't mind, I love being close to him, just not when he is telling me how he knows the world better than me. When I told him about my day at work he couldn't stop laughing. He gets a kick out of my stories about Brownie and the children. She is always fussing about something. He wasn't surprised to hear about the girl who was arrested either. He has been a correctional officer for the last 8 years and nothing seems to faze him. He is a man of the world, if you let him tell it.

"Babe, we see so many kids going to court in chains for murder, carjacking, drug selling, and even prostitution. You name it, they have done it," he said while cleaning the chicken for dinner.

"But babe she is 16 in the eighth grade and already has a record."

"She is 16, huh? She should be a junior in high school. That's common now a days. She's lucky. Some of the kids who get locked up won't see the outside world until they are our age. They have no future. At least she is getting another chance."

"Oh boy, don't say that around Brownie. She isn't keen on second chances."

"For instance, today we picked up a kid from court who is about 15, maybe 16 years old. He got 10 years for drug trafficking, armed robbery, and prostitution. When I asked him how he got caught up in this mess he told me his older brother got him hooked on ecstasy and he needed to support his habit."

"Wait a minute, did you say prostitution?"

"Yep, prostitution," he said grabbing a pan from under the counter.

"That's a shame, 16 and a drug addict going to jail for the next 10 years. He hasn't even begun living. See, that is exactly what I was trying to tell Brownie. So many kids won't get a second chance in the world. That is why we need to give them one in our classrooms. Sometimes we are the only people who will. Our students learn behaviors from us, too. You know my 'favorite' gave me a second chance today."

"Your favorite?" asked Calvin, putting the chicken in the pan.

"Yeah, my favorite. You know I told you before about my favorite… You know the little boy whose mom is sick, but comes to school every day in uniform, with his homework, and likes to read. You know who I am talking about?"

"Oh yeah, my competition," Calvin said, chuckling.

"Hush up," Willie says, pushing Calvin in his chest. "Yeah, well after the girl read her entry no one wanted to read. Can't really blame them. That was a hard one to follow. I was dying inside because I didn't know what to say after that. Anyway, he raised his hand and read his entry, so I would stop begging and looking pathetic."

"How is that a second chance? Sounds more like he saved the day," Calvin said, pretending to fly out of the kitchen like a superhero.

"He did. I needed a chance to get myself together. He knew it so he gave me a chance to do it. He is such a good student and a nice young man."

"I may have to watch out for him. He may steal your heart from me."

"No way, Babe. You've got all of me. He just has a special little place in my heart. But you've got all the rest. I promise."

Chapter Ten

The Boy

I couldn't wait to get home and tell my brother about the girl in class. That's if he is even home today. Her journal entry was hot because a hustler's life is cool. At least my brother makes it seem that way. She reminded me of him a little bit. He's been hustling for a while and hasn't gotten caught yet, unlike her. He is always geared up with a wad of money and gold fronts. He works for Mike Mike, like that girl use to, but he sells chocolate city heroin, not weed like she did.

My brother just turned 16 and is still in the eighth grade with me. He is one of the biggest kids in my class, but there are a couple other kids in there his age, too. He is in my English class, when he shows up for school, but he stopped coming altogether since Momma's sickness is getting worse. He stays home to take care of her. It is weird being in the same class as him because no one knows we are brothers because we have different last names. Only our two teachers know we are related, Mr. Mack and Ms. Wilson.

When he shows up for class we sit together and I help him. Not give him the answers or nothing like that, but I would read to him. My brother isn't a good reader. So, when we have a test in English, I sit next to him and read him the questions and he circles his answers. On like five tests we both got zeroes because Ms. Wilson thought we were cheating. I got tired of failing tests and told her what I was doing. She was cool with it and didn't say anything else about it. He didn't need my help in math because he was good at it so we didn't sit together in that class. He actually had a B in math until he stopped coming. It's only the three of us and he always makes sure we are good. He takes care of us. I know this is why he sells the "CC"… for money for us.

Momma's check is never enough to take care of all the bills. The lights were out and we couldn't even use the stove. They had been cut off a few times before. Sometimes we didn't have enough food for all of us to eat, but my brother always made sure me and Momma ate even if he didn't. We survived.

I remember the time our lights had been cut off for a few months in the summer; but we made it through the winter because they can't cut you off until March. In March and April, we had no lights. It snowed in March for a week. It was cold as shit. We ate cold cut sandwiches, Chinese carry-out, and chicken boxes. The house was lit with candles and flashlights at night. I would read the school novels or my brother's magazines by flashlight to have something to do since I couldn't watch TV. I loved going to school to get a hot lunch and some heat, if nothing else.

Things are different now. My brother is disappearing for days now. He hasn't been home to take care of Momma, so that means I am in charge and I have to stay home from school. And yep, our lights are out again. Our neighbors let us run an extension cord from their house to ours so I could run an electric heater for Momma so she wouldn't be so cold. They check on her, too, when I really need to go to school. This lasted about 2 weeks until they got their light bill and it was sky high. The extension cord hook up stopped. It has been 2 weeks and my brother hasn't been home. I am mad because I have only been to school like four or five times because I have to stay home with Momma. Then, today he comes home all geared up and says, "The BGE man is outside to hook us back up."

I looked at him like he was crazy because our bill was really high. I asked him where did he get the money? The bill was like $1000? He told me not to sweat it, he had it, and went to check on Momma upstairs.

I heard her ask him where he had been and then the door closed. They were arguing. Momma's voice sounded so weak and raspy compared to my brother's deep voice. She didn't need to be arguing and she didn't have the energy to do it, either. I was about to go upstairs when the lights came on. I jumped around and started dancing. I didn't even know my brother came back down stairs until he said, "what the fuck you doing?" shaking his head.

"Nothing."

"Whateva, I am going to the market to get some real food. What you want?"

"Yeah, some almond Smash soda, ice cream, cookies, and some pancakes..."

"Dag niggah, you want pancakes? Aight, clean out the fridge and dump the ice out the cooler. Be back."

I ran up to my momma's room to tell her the good news, but she was asleep, at least I thought she was until she mumbled something, nodding her head.

Momma was mumbling, laughing, and singing to herself… "I feel good, like I knew dat I would, umph, so good, so dayum good."

I watched her as she rocked her head back and forth singing. The room smelled funny like burnt metal. I looked around and that's when I saw a spoon and a lighter on top of the TV. Was Momma high? I looked at her again and my heart dropped. I stood there and watched, watched my momma sing herself to sleep. I walked closer to her and picked up the spoon and lighter. There was stuff still on the spoon. I tried to wipe it off, but it just smudged my uniform shirt. Why did he do this to her? She's our momma, not some trick off the streets. I just stood there and watched momma sleep or do a heroin nod, wondering if my brother was that fucked up in the head that he would make our momma a fein? I went back down stairs. I wanted to throw something, anything, but was scared of what I might break. I sat at the kitchen table mad as shit, waiting for my brother to get back from the market. About an hour later he came home.

"Yo, I know you probably hungry and shit so I brought you sumthin' good to eat," he said laughing. Stopped at Crazy Chicken and got you a chicken box and a half and half."

I didn't say anything.

"Oh yeah, I got ya cookies, soda, and your pancake mix, too," he said while smiling and looking in the bag.

I didn't say anything.

He looked up from the bag and said, "What da fuck is yo problem?"

I didn't say anything. He was my brother. He was supposed to be taking care of us. I didn't know what to say to him; so I raised the spoon and lighter. He looked away.

"Aww man, what?"

He started putting the food away real fast. "I'ma leave some money and I'll be back later."

"You gave Momma heroin?"

"Yo, mineya bizness, aight?"

"Momma is my business. You trying to make Momma a drug hoe," I yelled.

"Hell nah, I ain't tryin' to make Momma no ho! Don't get fucked up for real, watch ya mouf," he said getting angry.

"She's our momma, not one of those nasty tricks on the street you sell shit to. One of them hoes you get head from!"

"Women out in da streets are movah's, too," he said snickering.

"'Sides, I sell 'em dat shit 'cause they wanna get high. I don't care about dem bitches. Besides we would have never got our shit back on with me just selling weed."

"You don't care about Momma? Why you give it to her if you care about her?"

"Care? Man you don't get it! Did you hear what I just said?"

"Why you do it?" as I threw the spoon and lighter at him with tears rolling down my face. "Ain't she sick enough? She gonna die already. You want her to die sooner?" That was the first time I had said it out loud since we found out how sick Momma really was. We just stared at each other.

"You saw her, she didn't feel shit, but nice. I had to do something. Living here with no lights or heat. Shit, Momma is sick and hurting all the time. The medicine she is taking don't help her. She was hurting before. She ain't hurting nah," he said almost begging.

"What's all the noise down there, I'm trying to sing?" Momma yelled from her room, sounding stronger than before.

My brother walked by me saying, "We ain't yelling, Ma. Here I come. That shit make her feel better, so mind ya biz aight?" he said as he brushed past me going upstairs.

He disappeared upstairs and closed the door. My face was covered in tears, as I began to put the rest of the food away. When I opened the refrigerator's door I stepped on the lighter and noticed the spoon was gone.

My brother came down stairs and went straight out the door. I knew what he did. My tears dried up because I was mad as hell. I wanted to fight him, but knew I couldn't win. So I decided I was gonna check on Momma because I heard her calling.

Momma called out and started singing, nodding, eyes closed like the drug addicts I had seen on Harlem and Fulton or on Pennsylvania Ave. I went over to her and shook her. "Momma, you want something to eat? Mama?" She said nothing, just smiled.

CHAPTER ELEVEN

MS. BROWN

Friday's classes were nerve wracking. There must be a full moon or something because the kids are off. Some kids were louder than normal. The usual suspects were louder than normal and even the ones that are normally compliant were acting up, too. I almost checked the almanac on line and the lunch schedule because something was wrong with the school climate.

Willie even noticed that her favorite is changing, too. I watched him during class today and he had a far off look—that blank stare look. What was he thinking about? Willie said she would talk to him because I am too rough. I don't think I am rough, just real. Life experiences and exposure to certain things have made me tough and a pessimist. Taking ownership of bad situations like they are my own is something like making them my personal badge of womanhood, like a Girl Scout troop, except for women with issues. I think they are a reflection of me as a woman, I guess. I need to stop doing that.

Willie wants to talk to him because she wants to know what is going on with him. She can have that burden. I don't need to know. Did he do my work? Is it complete? Ownership, it's a reflection of me as teacher because the school system is data driven. The school system forces ownership on teachers; and the data is the cattle prod. Teaching is now a tug of war, a political game with teachers as scapegoats if schools do poorly. The politicians as the victors if schools do well. Data results mean demotion or declaration of my teaching ability and pay. That is my only concern. I have to hold my students accountable, if only to get some of my own back, because the school system is only interested in student progress as shown on paper. Other than that, I have no desire to know their issues. What happens during my 43 minutes of instruction in this classroom is my only concern. It has to be. It is the only protection I have against letting anybody get close to me.

I know I need to make some telephone calls. The little red-hair, freckled-face girl is not producing any work. She is definitely going to fail my class. Those little participation points I was going to give her wouldn't make any difference to her grade anyway. She is another one who sits there and just zones out. I don't care what Willie says, they just don't care about education. I'm wasting my time!

CHAPTER TWELVE

THE BOY

Momma is getting worse. Physically, she was bad, but I don't think she knew it because she was always high. My brother claimed that now he sells drugs to take away Momma's pain too, like he has to justify what he did to Momma. This meant that the beef between my brother and me didn't get any better, either. He tried talking to me, but I would just walk away, until one day we got a letter from my mother's brother. My Unk wanted us to know he was getting out of jail and that he was coming straight to us. He wanted to be here to take care of his baby sis and his nephews. I was so excited I ran to tell Momma, but she was asleep and that is when I heard the door. My brother was home, so I ran down the steps and ran up on him when he swung on me.

"Niggah, what da fuck you doing?"

"What the fuck you hit me for?" I asked rubbing my jaw.

"Yo, you don't run up on a niggah! Nevah, unless you ready to get fucked up!"

"You ain't have to hit me, dag."

"Shit, you ain't been speakin' to me for weeks and then you run up on me coming from upstairs, didn't know what to think."

We looked at each other for what seemed like forever, me rubbing my jaw and him looking sorry. Then I remembered why I had run down stairs in the first place.

"Unk's getting out. I got the letter today," I said as I handed him the folder piece of paper.

"Oh."

"Oh? Is that all you got to say? He is getting out and coming to stay with us. He wants to help take care of Momma."

"We don't need his help. I got dis."

"What ya sayn'? You don't want him to come stay with us?"

"I don't give a fuck, as long as he stay out my way," he said as he walked upstairs leaving the letter on the floor.

When Unk came about 2 weeks later things only got worse. Mom had been in and out of the hospital and my brother was mad all the time. Unk didn't look like he just got out of jail. He's about 6 feet tall with big muscles with "Dear Momma" tattooed on his neck. He had cut off his dreads and looked like one of my teachers all geared up. He didn't act like he just got out of jail, either, because not only did he have a car— that he never moved because there were few places to park—but money, too. It was like he hadn't been locked up for the last 2 years. I wanted to ask where he got all the money and the car from, but I didn't. I was scared. Momma always told us to stay out of grown folks business and that is what I did.

Unk came in and paid all the overdue bills, went to the market, and cleaned up the house. I went to school with clean uniform shirts and he would even try to help me with my homework. He wasn't much help with English and History, but Math was his thing just like my brother. Maybe that's why he had so much money when he got out of jail. My brother didn't stay home anymore. He only came around when Unk wasn't home "to take care" of Ma and he was out. My brother didn't want anything to do with him. He said Unk got soft and wasn't down anymore. He thought Unk was trying to come here and be somebody's daddy. He wasn't fuck'n with Unk and said that he was a joke, a clown.

My brother kept telling me, "he tryin' to run shit, but he ain't runnin' shit ova here. I'm a man! Best believe."

For that reason, Unk and my brother stayed out of each other's way for the most part. Unk had enough to deal with when Momma was admitted to the hospital, trying to explain why she had that shit in her system, and making sure I stayed in school at the same time. After a while, the hospital started sending over a nurse to check on Momma, and found out about Momma's "new medicine" my brother had been giving her. She threatened to call the police, but somehow Unk talked her out of it. My Unk was a smooth talker with the ladies. Too bad he couldn't talk his way out of jail or into a relationship with my brother. He wanted to build a relationship with my brother, get him out the game and off the streets, but he said my brother was old enough to know what he wanted so he wasn't gonna force himself on nobody.

Trying to focus on school work was getting hard because all I could do was think about Momma. Ms. Wilson noticed me zoning out in her class and told me she wanted to see me before I went home. I was gonna skip and go home, but Ms. Wilson was one of those teachers that would come to your house. So I decided to go.

CHAPTER THIRTEEN

MS. WILSON

I didn't even realize that he had been standing in the door because I was busy putting in grades until he called my name.

"Hey. Come on in and have a seat, son. Can we talk? Is everything okay?" He sat down and looked at the floor.

"Look at me, please." He lifted his head with eyes empty and sad. You want a snack or a soda?" I asked, opening my desk drawer. He shook his head no and just stared at me. "What has been going on in that head of yours? What's on your mind when you're in my class? I know it is not school work. Your thoughts are somewhere else."

At first he didn't say anything. I guess he was trying to get his thoughts together and then he started breathing hard. We had talked about his brother and his mom before. Maybe that's what was upsetting him. I had listened to him then, and had given him advice. Sometimes I gave him money for the snack line to make him feel better—maybe even special. Because I had worked hard to build a rapport, I hoped he would tell me the truth; so I waited while he stared at the floor again.

"I don't want to say it," he began with his eyes still on the floor.

"They just told me last night." His voice held on the slightest quiver. I felt for him. My own feelings rose in me like a submerged mirror to his own feelings. "If I say it out loud," he continued, glancing at the chalkboard behind me, "it would make it real and I don't want it to be real." His voice choked for a minute. "My mom is sick. Has been for a minute And she ain't gettin' no betta. She is getting worse!"

I almost said something, but then I stopped. I know I was going to correct him, but this was not the time for a paycheck vocabulary speech. Funny thing is, he did it for himself.

"I mean, she isn't getting any better."

I smiled and nodded looking into his eyes.

"Now they are taking her out of the hospital and putting her somewhere else, called a hos-pice, because they said there is nothing else they can do for her."

"Umm, oh, so they are going to put your mom in hospice?"

"Yeah that's what they said. What is that, a hos-pice?"

Whoa, what a question. Not the time to have a soap box moment on the importance of explaining information to children. Lord, give me the correct words. I took a breath and said, "hospice is a place where they take people who are very sick and try to make them as comfortable as possible before they pass away." God did that came out right? The look on his face broke my heart. He realized that the statement "there was no more they could do" meant his mom was going to die. There was nothing left to do but wait. Wait for his mother to die or wait for a miracle.

"I know this is difficult for you and…"

"What, so this place is where people go to die?" he said with a child-like innocence he had never displayed before. He stood up breathing loudly now.

"Wait. Let me explain, I do understand how you're feeling..."

"No you don't understand, Ms. Wilson. You have no fuck'n idea."

"Whoa, whoa just one second, yes I do understand. I lost my mom at 14," I said with too much emotion. "I know you're hurting and I wish there was something I could do to take the pain away." He looked again at me, with eyes—empty. I wasn't sure if it was what I said about the hospice or about the fact I had lost a parent, too. He was silent so I stayed silent, too.

"Aight Ms. Wilson, I gotta go," he said and turned around to leave.

"I am here if you need me, if you wanna talk or if..." he just raised his hand good-bye and walked out. I felt so helpless. I wanted to give him my cell number so if he wanted to call me and talk he could, but that was risky. A female teacher giving her number to a male student in this day and age is like going to jail without a trial. It leads others to believe the worst about the relationship. Can't blame them with how teachers are making the 11 o'clock news regularly.

I have heard those words before, "nothing more they can do for her." I wanted to hug him and tell him it would be alright. I know how it feels to lose a mother at a young age. My mom died when I was 14 and to this day, I still ache. I had my dad and my sisters to comfort me. We comforted each other and with them and God we made it through. I was strong because of them. How will he cope? Who will be there to support him? His brother is only a few years older than him and he is living a dangerous life. He doesn't come to school because he is hanging out on the corner of Fulton and Lafayette with some older men. I know he has seen me. He pretends to look right by me, but he knows I am there. Well, he can't ignore this. What will they do when their mom passes away?

I remember waiting for a miracle just like him. My miracle never came. God had taken her away. My mother's death was one of the hardest life changing events I ever encountered. It's like someone taking a breath before going underwater and never reaching the surface again for air. I was a floating spirit that would never rest because my anchor was cut away. I had been hollow for months looking for answers and asking God why. I needed an answer. My mommy didn't deserve this type of an end. She was too sweet, too kind, and too helpful to die like that. Why would God allow her to die in such a horrible manner? She missed birthdays, my graduation, my crossing the sands for Alpha Kappa Alpha. She will not be there when I get married or have my first child or when I need advice about being a good wife or mother. I didn't know how my sisters and I were going to learn how to be ladies with our mother gone? Yes, we had our Aunt Bobby, but the reality was she wasn't Mom, although she was the closest thing to her.

My older sister was left to fill Mom's shoes. She stepped up and sacrificed her teenage years to make sure my younger sister and I were cared for while Daddy worked. I wish she didn't have to, but I am so grateful she did. Will his brother be there to take care of him or this uncle, who he journals about, who has also just showed up out of the blue? Who is he really and where has he been all this time? Who is going to take care of him? Does he even believe in or know about God's grace?

"Hey Willie, you okay?" asked Brownie, peeking inside the classroom door. "I just saw your favorite walking down the hall. He looked so pitiful."

"Yeah, it's just one of those days when you ask yourself why this profession?"

"I know, but just admit it; we can't get away from these kids. Something makes us stay. Perhaps it is in our blood. Besides, we were both crazy from the start and this is how we stay sane," Brownie said laughing. "You want a soda? I am on my way to the vending machine. I hope it's working. I need the caffeine, since I can't have a drink."

"Yeah, you can get me anything. I appreciate it."

"Okay, be back in a minute. We can talk about what's going on with him and why he's driving you crazy, and making you question your career choice."

"Alright," I said smiling. I stared at the computer. I couldn't focus on putting grades in so instead I decided to pray. "God, please give that little boy strength to face the trials that will follow. Help him seek out and be sought out for support and comforting. Don't let him get caught up in the wrath of the streets. Lord, I don't know if I can handle losing another student to the streets. Keep him safe, Lord. Amen."

Chapter Fourteen

Ms. Brown

Willie and I think so much alike. It's funny how we are both asking ourselves the same question. 'Cause after today, I am not sure why I teach, either. Can we really help these children? It seems like I ask myself this question every day. Maybe I need to get into another profession. I am still trying to figure out my own life. Do I want to figure out theirs, too? I got my own problems. If I wanted to deal with children issues, I would have had one of my own or have been a child physiologist.

I truly don't understand what is wrong with these children. They don't respect adult authority. Everything is a debate. Administrators and counselors claim teachers know what type of issues or baggage students bring into their classroom. For real—what issues do they really face? They live rent free, get name brand clothes, high priced cell phones, and money. Meanwhile, I am here late most evenings creating lessons for students who don't do homework or class work. Ungrateful bastards! It is so depressing. Oh, I need a drink! Unfortunately, I am still here, so I will have to settle for some caffeine.

Just as I dropped off Willie's soda I was paged by Mrs. Johnson, our school secretary, over the intercom. Apparently, I need to report to the conference room as well as take a call on extension 0826. I decided to take the call first and then report to this last minute, unscheduled meeting in the conference room. As if I didn't have anything else to do besides wait around for impromptu meetings all day. I was ready to go home and didn't feel like being bothered. No one bothered to take my time into consideration; therefore, I will take my time getting to this meeting. I greeted Mrs. Johnson when I entered the office and asked her if I could use the telephone at her desk. She nodded yes and I picked up the receiver.

"Good afternoon. This is Ms. Brown," I said as professional and polite as possible for a 3:30 telephone call, 45 minutes after the end of my work hours.

"Ah, yes. *Ms. Brow*. Good afternoon. I am calling because my son tole me you took his cell phone today during seventh period and I am calling to see when I can come and get it," said the voice on the other end.

Wow. I have been trying to meet with this parent for two quarters now. She has yet to respond to my parent conference requests, but she calls today about her son's $200 cell phone. Ain't that some shhhhhhh. I have called this woman I don't how many times about her son's behavior and lack of academic progress and she calls today—not to discuss his academics, but because I took his damn phone.

"I paid almost $300 for dat phone and he needs to get it back."

"Well ma'am, he was sending a text message during class and the school policy clearly states that…" I hold the telephone away from me as shouting arises on the other end. Even Ms. Johnson can hear as the parent rants.

"Who in da hell you text'n while you was in *Ms. Brow's* class?" This was surely shouted into the receiver for my benefit or as some token of discipline.

"It is Ms. Brown ma'am."

"Oh, I am so sorry Ms. Brown. It won't happen again," she said louder than anything else she had said. "I will be up dere tomorrow morning before I go to work to get da phone, okay?"

"Okay," I said annoyed. "Well ma'am since we are on the telephone I would also like to talk to you about his academic progress in my class." Before I could even begin to explain that he is not completing homework or class work the famous speech began.

"I know, I know *Ms. Brow*, he ain't been doing what he suppose to be doing in ya class. I told him he is in the eighth grade now and he gotta do it on his own. I can't make him do it, so if he fail, then he fail. I can't afford to take off work to come up to dat school 'cause he wanna act a fool. So you do what you gotta do, *Ms. Brow*. He will learn sooner or later. Well thank you for your time. I will talk to him again. I will be dere in the morning to get his phone."

"Okay and thank you," I said totally annoyed now.

"And you have a blessed week *Ms. Brow*. Thank you."

I hung up even more annoyed and irritated. Have a blessed week my behind! I was not surprised. How many times have I heard this speech since I started teaching? That is what some parents say until it's time to prepare for the eighth grade promotion ceremony. Then let the show begin. The questions flood the office like a river after a torrential rain. So what can he do to participate? Nothing. Are there any extra credit assignments he can do to make up? No. Can he do all the work from this quarter to bring up his grade? Oh, HELL NO! I don't think it's fair to my other students who have worked hard all year to have some student do 10 weeks of work at the 13th hour. Then here it comes, the big one. Well, I don't think it's fair to punish him like dat. He is just a child, who needs guidance and a second chance. After teaching 11 years, you would think that this question would no longer baffle me—it does. I still can't believe it. Weren't you the one who said he had to do this on his own? Now you want to blame the teacher for his short comings? Hell, isn't that your child? But you can't say that and maintain professionalism. So what do you do except stay quiet and teach? Humph… While I'm thinking about it, I need to call the group home about the red hair, freckled-face girl and her lack of homework submissions. Nah, I will do it tomorrow. I don't think I can deal with anything else. I walked out the office.

Ms. Johnson giggled and said, "Don't forget about the meeting in the conference room, Brownie."

"Auggghhh! I just wanted to go home, Ms. Johnson," I said as I turned around to walk down the hall. "I'm going, I'm going."

CHAPTER FIFTEEN

The Red-hair, Freckled-face Girl

Dear Diary,

I had my session with that Ms. Betty lady and she seems cool. She wanted to know how school was going and before I got a chance to tell her she tole me don't lie. Dayum, she saw right through me. I was gonna tell her some real shit, but guess not cause she said she be talking to my counselor at school. So I told her da truth. No I don't be doing my homework and a lot of times I don't be doing my class work either. I looked at her like now what? She dug right into to me. She asked me if I wanted to go home or stay here. I wanna go home. Well she said I ain't going home til I get my act together in school and complete the therapy sessions the courts want me to do. She tole me about the activities they have and they sound cool. So if I wanna have some fun like skating, going to da movies, and da mall I gotta act right here and at school.

She tole me I was being put on a progress sheet and

all my teachers would have to sign it every day telling her about my work and behavior. Dayum, that messes up my whole program of getting on Ms. Ugly Brown's nerves. Then she asked was there anything else I wanted to talk about?... If I wanted to talk about what happened at the house the night I was taken away? I tole her nope. She say I gotta talk about it sooner or later or I won't be going home. Shit, I guess it will be lata. I took my progress sheet and I was out. When I left I was going back to my room when dis new girl was moving in. She is tall as hell with long black hair. She is cute and mean looking all at da same time with her black lips and nails. Maybe she is one of those goth kids. She looked me dead in my face and kept going. I don't know what she did to be put in here, but she don't look like she is to be fucked wit.

CHAPTER SIXTEEN

Ms. Brown

I walked into the conference room to find Mr. Allen, the science teacher, and Mr. Mack, the math teacher, already at the table looking as happy as I did about this unscheduled meeting.

"Good afternoon gentlemen," I said when I entered the conference room.

"Hey Brownie," said Mr. Allen.

"Good afternoon, how ya doing Brown," replied Mr. Mack as I sat down next to him.

"Does anyone know what we are going to discuss this afternoon in this last minute, end-of-the-day-I-was-on-my-way-home meeting?" asked Mr. Allen.

"Nope, and I have papers to grade," said Mr. Mack.

"Aren't interims coming out next week?" asked Mr. Allen.

"Dag that quick? Already that time?" asked Mr. Mack taking out a stack of papers and a pen.

"Oh, it's the most wonderful time of the year. The time of year when you are called everything, but your government name. Has anyone been called out their name today or are we all safe until interims are handed out?" I said chuckling.

We all laughed because no one is exempt from a child trying to go off on you and calling you out of your name. We all gave a church—umm humm—and laughed.

"Well, to make it easy for me, I am giving everybody a C," said Mr. Allen, pushing his glasses up on his nose. "I don't feel like the drama, we are already in the third quarter." Mr. Allen was a mahogany colored man with an egg shaped head. He always wore a tie to work with the same brown shoes. He was one of the shorter men in our building with a Napoleon complex to boot, but loved teaching. He did experiments in his Science class that students would talk about weeks after they were completed. I thought he was cute in a nerdy sort of way, especially with his bible tucked under his arm.

"You can do that if you want Al, but I am not giving away a grade," chimed in Mr. Mack. Mr. Mack was a 6 foot 6, peanut butter colored man who wore our school polos and khakis everyday like the kids. He believed if he wore the uniform as an example the children wouldn't complain about them as much. Mr. Mack believed that every child could learn, most of the time.

"I work too hard to do that. I left the corporate world because of foolishness like that... Shoot, people giving bonuses and promotions to people who accomplish nothing. I enjoy watching the kids when they finally understand a concept. That light bulb over their head shining brightly effect keeps me going," he said while looking up at the ceiling.

I smiled as I looked at these two men who loved teaching. They had a passion for education that I have never experienced. I need to find a career to make me feel like that, because teaching doesn't.

After some additional idle chitchat the eighth-grade guidance counselor, Mrs. Woodrow, and the eighth-grade assistant principal, Mrs. Harris, came into the conference room and sat down across from each other. After quick salutations, Mrs. Woodrow informed us that we were here to discuss the red-hair, freckled-face girl whose residence I was just about to call.

"We all know that she lives in a group home and has for some time now," said Mrs. Woodrow. We all nodded our heads in offering that this is common knowledge.

"But, we have finally received all her records and there are some delicate issues that you, as her teachers, should be aware of," she said staring meaningfully at Mr. Mack who was grading papers.

"She was removed from her home because she was being abused by her mother's boyfriend." Mr. Mack stopped grading papers and gave Mrs. Woodrow his full attention like the rest of us. I guess before we were all thinking the same thing, but before anyone could ask the question she answered it.

"Yes, sexually abused by her mother's boyfriend."

"So they put *her* out of the house?" asked Mr. Mack with disgust. "What kind of judicial system do we trust in where they just put the child out of the house?"

"Well, that's not all Mr. Mack," said Mrs. Woodrow with a sigh. "They put her out of the house because she began to molest her younger brother."

You could hear everyone gasp at the same time before the questions began to fill the room.

"They put her out and left the boyfriend there?" inquired Mr. Allen.

"What does her mother think about this?" I asked.

"Wait a minute. The boyfriend got away with it? Are there any other children in the house besides her and the brother? How do they know that he won't do it to them?" responded Mr. Mack.

"Wait guys, I know, I know. There is still more for me to tell you."

"I don't think I want to hear anymore," said Mr. Allen wiping his face with his hand, readjusting his glasses.

"Well, since she has been out of the home she is under constant supervision, which brings us to the reason for this emergency meeting. The advisors at the home believe that she may be at risk of being a repeat offender; therefore, she cannot leave your classroom without adult supervision. No bathroom passes, nurse passes, or office passes should be distributed to her unless you can physically walk her to her destination. The staff at the group home has advised us that she is not to be left alone with other students because they are not sure of what she may do."

"She has been going all this time and now she can't go? What if she needs to go to the restroom during class and it's an emergency?" I asked.

"Well that is why we are here," said Mrs. Harris. We need to set up a time when she can use the restroom and an adult is present when she goes."

"Oh wow! How in the heck can we keep a child from going to the restroom?" asked Mr. Allen.

"It has to be done for her safety and the safety of the other students," Mrs. Harris interjected.

"What I suggest is that she goes to the nurse's suite to use the rest room. Unfortunately, the only time a teacher can walk her there is during lunch time. So, she can use the restroom before and after lunch in the nurse's suite. If there is an emergency then call the office and I will come and take her," said Mrs. Woodrow. "This is going to seem strange because I do lunch duty. I give students' passes to the restroom all the time. It is going to be weird telling one student no while everyone else can go. It's a shame because it's not her fault. But it is what we have to do. Ms. Brown, since you have her before lunch you can drop her off at the nurse's suite. Ms. Brown? Ms. Brown, are you with us?" asked Mrs. Woodrow.

"Yeah, I am just thinking about this poor little girl, that's all." I shook my head in disbelief; astonished that this had happened to this girl. She didn't look like the type, but neither did I.

Chapter Seventeen

The Boy

After talking to Ms. Wilson today, I came straight home. What a fucked up day! First, I find out what it really means to be in a hospice, and then I come home and walk in on Unk and his boys jerking off downstairs in the basement. I just came up to the room that I share with my brother, who is always gone, and turned on the TV. I still can't believe what I had just seen—it was so nasty. I sat on my bed when I heard footsteps coming up the stairs. I thought it was my Unk, but it was the man with the purple bag.

"Yo Shorty, why you leave?"

"I ain't wanna see dat shit," I said flipping channels, wondering why the hell he was in my room. I hope he washed his hands.

"Oh you don't watch flicks?" as he put his hands on top of his head.

His zipper was undone and I saw it, his thang was poking out a little. I shook my head and turned back towards the TV.

"Ah, you jumped like a biotch. You ack like you ain't nevah seen a dick befo'," he laughed.

I ignored him because he was high and drunk, but ignoring him just seemed to irritate him.

"Yo, Shorty, you hear me talking to you? Don't be disrespeckin' me. I knew your uncle up Jessup and I can spank dat ass if need be," he said sucking his teeth.

He was walking towards me with his hand on his belt. I don't know why he had on a belt because it wasn't holding up his pants.

"Yo, you look like dis faggy boi who would take care of me up Jessup. You got big lips like him, too," he said while grabbing his stuff. "He would suck my shit for me like my girl used to before I got locked up."

I tried to concentrate on the TV and not put my hand over my mouth, but he came and stood right in front of it.

"Yep, just like dat faggy boi. You jumped like a faggy boi, too" he said chuckling.

"I ain't no faggy," I said with the hardest voice I could. "I don't fuck with no boys. I gets at the ladies. Know what I'm sayn'?" as I tried to stand up.

"Sit yo ass down," he said as he pushed me back down by my shoulders. "Yo, I ain't gay. Shit. I put it down on my Shorty," he said backing away. "What happened up in Jessup is survival, son. You go crazy up there. A bunch of dudes, no girl, you get some pics, if the COs don't take 'em out ya mail. But I'm all man, know what I'm sayn'?"

He sat down next to me, his pants still unzipped. I tried to relax, but he smelled awful and he was too close. We sat in silence for a while when he grabbed a pillow and laid back with his eyes closed. I glanced at his thang. It was poking out again.

"You lookin' at my shit? You'se a faggy boi," he said laughing. "Ahhh, little man looking at my dick. You look at boys in school, too, don't ya?"

"Hell nah, I gets girls all the time," I said as I got up to walk to the door.

"Yo, where you going?"

"Oustide," I said. I didn't care what I said as long as I was not in this room with him.

"Oh, you hustle? Going out to make dat paper?" he said sitting up.

"Nah, Unk would kill me. He don't want me to get locked up like he did so he makes sure I get what I want so I don't have to. But my brother does," I said with pride.

"Word? Ya brotha do, huh? But what about you? I know ya Unk can be slow wit given up money. So I know fo sho you ain't getting paid like you could. So how 'bout it? You wanna make $20 real fast?" he said looking me in my eyes sucking his teeth.

"Yeah," I said, not thinking about anything I just said or what my Unk would do to me. "What you want me to do? Deliver a package, be a look out, be a duffle bag boy—what?"

He looked around the room, looked at me with his head tilted, and then he smiled. "None of dat shit you talking 'bout. Come here."

I didn't like the way he said "come here." Made me feel—I don't know. I didn't feel right. I saw it again. His thang wasn't just poking out anymore, it was out. I stood and looked at him not sure what to do.

"Yo, you wanna make $20 or what?" he asked again.

"Yeah, I guess. What I gotta do?"

"You guess? Yo, here's da deal. You finish me off for interrupting me downstairs and I will give you $20."

"Huh?" My eyes widen as I watched him rub his thang. My mouth dropped open, in shock, and he laughed saying, "you ain't ready for dat yet."

"Just rub it and jerk it 'til I bust. Take you 5 minutes and you make $20."

He took a large roll of money out of his pocket and laid the $20 bill next to him. I stood there thinking this is gay. It's nasty. I started shaking my head no, but then he pulled out another 20 and laid it next to the first one.

"Come on dude quit stalling. Either you is or you ain't. This is like your own hustle, but you ain't gotta worry 'bout no police... it's just us."

"My own hustle, like my brother, but I won't get shot at or go to jail. I would have my own money and wouldn't have to wait for Unk to give me none," I half asked, half stated. Convincing myself it was just a hustle, nothing wrong with it.

He smiled at me and nodded yeah saying, "whateva, Lil' Shorty." He laid back, one arm above his head on the pillow.

"Aight then, bet," I walked over to him.

He zipped his pants up and was about to give me dap when he realized that my hand was full. I couldn't believe what I just did. I sat there with his human glue sliding through my fingers onto my pants leg.

"Aight Lil' Shorty. I'll holla," and he began to walk out the room.

I looked down and there was another $20 bill lying on the bed, $60 instead of $40. It was like he read my mind because he turned around and said, "a lil' something extra for a tip" and closed the door.

I felt the tears roll down my cheek. I wanted to wipe my face, but realized that I still had his cum in one hand and in the other hand, the money he left balled up in my fist. What had I done?

Chapter Eighteen

Ms. Brown

It is not her fault, it is not her fault, it is not my fault, it was not my fault, it was not my fault.

My face was against the wall and he was fingering me and humping me at the same time. I still smelled his saliva on my face because of the nasty first French kiss I received from my 15-year-old cousin. I wanted to cry, but the tears just wouldn't fall. He held me tighter and pumped so hard that my head began to hit the wall. I felt nasty. Why was he doing this to me? He was holding me so tight that my underwear were beginning to cut into me because he had moved them to one side. He pressed my face closer to his so I wouldn't make any noise and suddenly stopped. Something wet was between my butt cheeks.

"You betta not tell nobody either," he said breathing hard and zipping up his pants.

All I could do was shake my head yes.

"You say anything, I'ma tell you pulled up ya skirt and showed me your pussy. Ya momma will beat ya ass."

My cousin left the room and didn't look back. I pulled my underwear out of my behind and felt something slimy on my hand. I hurried and pulled my skirt back down. I looked at myself in the mirror that hung right next to where my cousin had just dry humped me and cried. I wondered did the bastard enjoy looking at himself take advantage of an 11 year old or couldn't he stand the sight of himself? For a long time after that I had a problem looking at myself in the mirror.

As I walked back to my classroom, all I could think about was innocence lost, hers and mine. She doesn't even look like the type—a child molester at the age of 12. The truth is, you can't look at a person and tell if they are beating their wife, being beat by their husband, molesting a child or being molested, considering suicide, or anything. The truth is no one knew that I was being molested and my parents where in the same house when it happened. That doesn't make them bad parents because I know if my dad ever found out he would have killed the son of a bitch. It just meant that molesters were sneaky and very manipulative. It would be so much easier if they wore jackets that said, "I am an abuser." That is why I am such an observer. It's a shame this girl's life is already screwed up because she wasn't protected. No wonder she just stares at me, her mind is dealing with issues outside her age comprehension level. What problems could a 12- to 15-year-old face that would merit the disrespect they show adults? Now I know. I guess I always knew.

CHAPTER NINETEEN

THE BOY

The man with the purple bag started coming by on a regular for the next couple of weeks. I'd get my "hustle on" as he called it and he left more money with each visit. I guess I was like my brother; I did it for the money. At first, I was saving my money, but then I thought why not buy some new gear? So I went to Security Mall and bought some jeans, shirts, and a new pair of tennis. The kids at school began to notice my new clothes and said stuff like somebody got some money, somebody getting their hustle on. I would just smile. Even my English teacher, Ms. Wilson, noticed. One day in the hall she said, "You haven't been in uniform. What happened?"

"Other people ain't wearin' it, so why should I?"

Ms. Wilson just shook her head and kept it moving. I couldn't tell her the truth. She wouldn't understand. So the best thing for Ms. Wilson to do was to mind her biz.

Besides, today I knew the man with the purple bag was coming over and I was hyped. I was about to get ready. I would wash my hands real good and greased them with Vaseline and lotion to make them slippery. As I waited on the porch trying not to touch anything this other man walked up on me, scared the shit out of me so I jumped.

"Yo, you Lil' Shorty?" he called out.

"Huh? Who? Why you asking?" I replied trying to sound hard.

"Trey sent me. Told me you nice wit ya hands," he said moving closer to me, whispering.

"Trey? I don't know no Trey. Who you talking about?" I thought about it for a minute and realized Unk had called one of his friends Trey. "The man with the purple bag?"

"The purple bag?" he said laughing. "He does drink Crown Royal all day. Yeah, him. He couldn't come today. Said I could instead. Told me you real good wit ya hands. When your uncle left, Trey was my celly up in Jessup. We real cool," he said leaning in close and looking around.

"So what dat got to do with me?"

"Don't ack stupid. You wanna make da money or not? Trey said you charge $20, what up?"

"Nah, I charge 60," I said surprising myself.

"Fuck dat! I can get a whole bid from a bitch for 60 bones," he said and began to walk away.

"Your loss. I'm good wit mines." I couldn't believe I just said that. I'm tripping. He turned around and smiled.

"Oh yeah? You cocky lil' niggah. Aight, let's go. Where you gonna do dis?"

"I got a spot. Let's go," I said leading him into the house.

After I was done, he left a hundred on my bed and told me to keep my mouf closed and my hands tight—and was gone. I didn't know why he left so much money, but I didn't care. I guess I was that good.

Two days later the man with the purple bag came over. I wasn't ready when he came by because I hadn't washed my hands yet.

"Hey Lil' Shorty, what up? I heard you set my man up right. Good looking out," he said, while handing me a $50 bill.

I wanted to ask him why he sent that man and again it was like he was reading my mind because he answered me before I could ask.

"Yo, he's real good people. He had my back up Jessup. We been cool ever since. You're a hustla' now, so you need customers. So I thought I'd hook you up."

I smiled because he called me a hustla'.

"You ready to do this?"

I nodded yes.

"Let's go then. I ain't got all dayum day."

When we got upstairs he went to my bedroom like he lived here. I went towards the bathroom to wash my hands.

"Where da fuck you going now?" he asked annoyed. "Why you always going some dayum where? Always leavin' and shit?"

"Gonna wash my hands," I said proudly.

"Nah, come on, you good. I trust ya," he said smiling.

"But I gotta…"

"I said come on. Shit, it's cool."

I turned around and went back towards the bedroom. He waited for me to go in first. He came in after me and closed the door. Then I smelled it. He smelled like liquor and weed. I sat on the bed, but he didn't. He was looking out the window.

"Lil' Shorty, you wanna make some real money?"

"Hell yeah!"

"Then you gotta up your game. A real hustla know dat when his product is good, he ups the cost and makes it even betta. So it's time to make ya hustle betta."

"Better? How do I do dat? I like the money I make now."

"See, you think small. A real hustla gotta always make sure he is two steps ahead of the next niggah. Like me, shit I make sure my shit always give da best and longest high. Other niggahs can't fuck wit me. I get new customers every day 'cause my shit is like dat. Know what I'm sayn?"

"Yeah, but how do I do dat?"

"Okay, let me school ya real quick. You gotta up ya game, son. Give'em sumthing betta everytime."

"Okay. Like what?"

"You really wanna know? You down?" he said rubbing his hands together and sucking his teeth.

"I'm down," I said nodding my head.

"You sure?"

"I'm fo sho."

He smiled and said "aight, cool." He stood in front of me, and unzipped his pants, and took out his thang. It stood straight up in my face. I looked at him with my mouth closed tight and my eyes open wide.

"You said you were down, right? This is gonna be hot! I told ya you had lips like dat faggy boi," as he grabbed his thang with his right hand and grabbed the back of my head with his left.

"What the FUCK!" My face was sticky and I wanted to throw up. Why do my cheeks hurt? I pushed him out of the way and ran to the bathroom. I turned on the water and began to wash my face when I realized the shit wouldn't come off. "It won't come off! It won't come off," I screamed in horror.

The man with the purple bag came in and said, "Chill out, Shorty, use a rag and wipe it off. Ya dumb fuck," he said and walked out laughing.

I scrubbed my face like I wanted to take my skin off. Got some mouth wash and gargled, spit, gargled, spit, gargled, and spit until I was tired. I sat on the toilet because I didn't want to see 'em. I was hoping he was gone. If this is gonna be my hustle, then fuck that shit. I felt like I was choking and gagging for real. I felt like a bitch, but I refused to cry like one. I got up a few minutes later and went into my room. He was gone. There was $200 lying on the bed. My hustle had changed.

Chapter Twenty

Ms. Wilson

"Put up your chairs! Hey, no going out in the hall before the—," the bells sounds before I can get the words out of my mouth. Whew, another day done. Thank you, Jesus.

As I review the day's work in order to prepare for tomorrow's lesson, I notice that I am missing my favorite student's work. It is not just today's work that is missing, either. His grades are awful. He has one, two… five missing assignments. He is too smart for that. He is changing more and more every day. He used to wear a uniform every day, but now its name brand shirts and new tennis shoes. God, I hope he's not hustling. Humph! He even got an earring. He barely does his class work and his homework is non-existent.

Calvin said that I was getting too attached and that I needed to step back some. Calvin thinks he is trying to deal with his situation in his own way. Not everyone grew up like us. I know that, but how can I ignore his change in behavior when I know he has so much potential? Brownie is even noticing it, too. She told me he is beginning to pick on other students in her class with his new best friend, the Boy with the Mohawk.

He hasn't really talked to me since we discussed his mom going to the hospice. I wonder how she is doing? I saw him in the hall and he blew me off! He even had the audacity to get smart with me! Me—the one who has had the best interest at heart all this time, he gets smart with me. No one has heard much about his mom or his brother lately. His brother hasn't been to school in months. So who is taking care of him? That "Unk" is, I guess. Maybe I will talk to Mrs. Woodrow about his change in behavior. Maybe she can help. If it doesn't get any better, I am going to call the uncle. I don't even want to think about the situation anymore until I get some definite information.

"Oh dag it, look at the time. I have been here all this time mulling over this boy. And now I am talking to myself. Let me gather these papers and get myself home."

Chapter Twenty-One

Ms. Brown

Lately, during fourth period I have began to feel uneasy. I know that in a few minutes she will be coming to my class and I can't show her that I now know her secret. She has been carrying a daily progress sheet, the ones that are used to keep students on track and serves as a communication device between teacher and parent. To me, these sheets are a waste of time. It seems like administrators hand them out like candy to every child that gives a teacher a problem. We are told they are used to encourage positive behavior, to me, another tree died for nothing. The sheets don't solve their problems, mediation does that.

She didn't need a sheet. She needed help. She thinks she is carrying the sheet to encourage her to do and pass in her homework, but I know it is for another reason. Mrs. Woodrow needs to monitor her movement and academic progress and it is a report for her counselor at the group home. My perspective has changed about this girl and I was struggling with her reality and trying to forget my own.

When the bell rings, the students enter the room full of good mornings and laughter. She is quiet as usual. She walks in, gives me her progress sheet, and sits in her assigned seat. I can't stop staring at her. I want to hug her, tell her I understand, and that she can trust me. We both have the same secret. That compassionate feeling is new for me because, normally, I don't care. Unfortunately, I can't hug her because she doesn't even know that I know. Since I can't hug her, I give myself a hug while standing at the door and then I went into the classroom. I can do this. At least she is out of the abusive situation, but damn the judicial system and her momma for blaming and punishing her. To me, the city has failed her by putting her out of the home and not arresting that trifling ass mother for not protecting her daughter and for not putting the boyfriend *under* the jail. Alright Brownie. Get it together, you've got a job to do.

"Good morning," I say as I started instruction. I am an emotional wreck with my spirit in pieces and staring at her while I went over the agenda for the day. For a minute, I don't think she was paying attention. I can't stop wondering what she is thinking about. As the students begin their class work, it looks like she is reading, but I am not sure. Her paper has been blank for the last 10 minutes and she hasn't picked up that pen yet. Maybe I will go over there by her and she will get started. When I walk over to where she is sitting, she doesn't move. Some of the kids started to giggle because she doesn't even notice I was behind her. I give them a look and the giggling stops. I touched her shoulder and she jumped and screamed.

"Don't touch me!"

She almost jumped out of her seat. Two boys, Willie's favorite and the Boy with the Mohawk, laugh and made a comment about her jumping. I look at them and they put their heads back in their books. She turned around, breathing hard, and staring at me in horror. The look she gives me catches me off guard. I realized touching her was not the best of ideas. It's just something teachers do to either give encouragement or queue a child to get focused and to start working. I should have known better. All I could say was, "Sweetie, you need to get started. I am collecting this at the end of class." I knew why she didn't want me to touch her. I wouldn't want to be touched, either. I didn't like being touched or hugged from behind. It made me feel unclean. I know how it feels to be trapped in an unwanted embrace in the body and the mind.

Chapter Twenty-Two

The Red-hair, Freckled-face Girl

Dear Diary,

Tonight in my session I had to tell Ms. Betty about me yelling in Ms. Brown's class. She thought it was about me going to the bathroom and I tole her no. I didn't know what she was talking about so I just tole her that was doing good. That seemed to make her happy and then I went on with my story.

Today in class, Ms. Brown was staring at me and it fucked wit my head. I couldn't figure out why she was staring at me. I didn't do anything. I spit my gum out before I even came to her class, so she didn't have to tell me to do that and I even did her work today. But she kept staring at me. I thought maybe she knew that today was my birthday, but she didn't say nuttin' about it. She just kept looking at me all crazy.

I tole Ms. Betty how sorry I was for yelling at Ms. Brown and she seemed okay with that. She asked to see my progress report. Ms. Betty wanted to know why

I yelled and I tole her I didn't like being stared at or touched anymore since he...

I remember when I was waiting for my mother to come home to take me shopping. I was watching T.V. and waiting like foreva. I watched Big Boy, my mother's new fat ass boyfriend, walk back and forth, drinking a beer, staring at me, and we both waited. He wanted to know why I was sittin' way on the other side of the room and he came and sat by me.

I ain't say nuttin'. I just pretended to be watching TV. He tole me I looked real cute in my jeans and that he didn't know I was dat thick. I didn't think I was phat, but he did. ☺ He wanted to know what I'd been eating to get phat ass thighs and then he rubbed me on my thigh. I flicked his hand off me and tole him not to touch me. He thought I was ackin' funny and tole me he wasn't gonna do nuttin' to my hot ass. He was just sayn' I was growin' up to be kinda cute. Shit, I was glad somebody thought I was cute. Nobody at school be tryin' to holla at me. The boy I like is hanging with that Boy with the Mohawk. I know he ain't thinkin' bout me. The cute girls in my class is who he be tryin' to holla at and he is gettin' em to. Oh yeah don't let me forget to tell you about the new girl.

Anyway, so he was like we cool and I was like yeah, and then he moved closer to me putting his arm around me for a second. Before I knew it he was rubbing my leg again sayin' I was phat and askin' did I have a boyfriend. I didn't like him rubbing on me and staring at me so I flicked his hand off again. He said I was ackin' all scary and shit, like ain't no body rubbed me before. The truth was nobody had rubbed me anywhere and then I didn't want to talk anymore. So I stopped. Ms. Betty just wrote down some notes and said okay we will talk later. She tole me happy birthday and gave me a cup cake with some bullshit candle on top. I gave her a fake ass smile and I left. I didn't tell her about the new girl so I will tell you.

☺ The new girl who moved into the home has been staring at me to, but I like the way she stares at me. She even said happy b-day to me when we was in the dining hall. She seem cool as shit. Wonder what's up wit her. When I find out I will let you know.

CHAPTER TWENTY-THREE

THE BOY

My hustle is blowing up. I have three customers now, the man with the purple bag, his friend from Jessup, and the guy from the basement, the one who busted when I interrupted their "little party." He is Unk's boy, too. The hand jobs are for the other two dudes, but the "specialty" as the man with the purple bag calls it, is only for him. My hustle is tight. I don't feel like I am choking anymore and I got good at cleaning myself off after, too. My gear is tight, and I am hanging with the Boy with the Mohawk at school who gets the hot girls and now the hot girls are trying to holla at me. Shit, I am popular. I am wearing all the latest shit, fuck that clown ass uniform. I am fresh with my gear and my pierced ear. Ms. Wilson doesn't like it, I could tell, but fuck her, too. I don't stay home as much, unless my customers came around. They come on certain days, 'cause real hustlas got a schedule. At least that is what the man with the purple bag said. Time is money. Don't waste time and you won't miss making any money. He said that if he continues to get me more customers, he's gonna have to start charging me a finder's fee. I was like nope I am good. I learned how to up my game on my own by watching some of my Unk's flicks for my "specialty". My shit is on lock, but everything else is fucked up. Momma is dying and Unk and my brother hate each other. My brother doesn't come to the house at all now and I wonder if he even knows Momma got so bad that they came and moved her into that hospice place.

I am going to school every now and then because I don't see the point. My mind is on Momma and my money. I can't focus on school work and Ms. Wilson is on my ass. Dayum.

CHAPTER TWENTY-FOUR

Ms. Brown

It has been a couple of weeks and I've noticed a big change in her behavior. The progress sheet is helping, I guess. I was receiving some homework and class work, not always correct, but it was handed in and it is more than I used to get. She even raised her hand to read aloud one day, which totally shocked me. Interestingly enough, she never asked to go to the restroom. I have offered to walk her to the nurse's suite if she needed to go, but she always looked at me like I was crazy and said no quietly. After a while, I stopped asking her if she needed to go. I assumed she was going after lunch. During class, she seemed attentive and focused on trying to do better, and I was pleased. She seemed happy for once and I was trying to help her stay that way until today…

She was working on a journal entry and asked to go to the bathroom. I looked at her and said no. She really looked like she needed to go, but no one was available to take her. Mrs. Woodrow was out today and Mrs. Harris was in a conference. I was in the middle of instruction and couldn't just leave to take her. She was going to have to wait. So she sat there very still and stopped working. After about 10 minutes, it was time to line up and she went toward the end of the line when Willie's favorite, who hadn't been to school in about a week, started pointing and laughing. The Boy with the Mohawk was with him and started laughing, too. The rest of the class had already started walking down the hall when I went back there to see what was going on. I looked at them and then looked at her and she put her head down with pity. The back of her pants were bright red. I told her to have a seat and asked Willie to walk my class the rest of the way to the cafeteria. I pulled the boy and his friend to the back and we went to Vegas. You know "what happens in Vegas, stays in Vegas." Sometimes I have to tell these little heathens off for them to understand where I'm coming from and I can't always do that with an audience. I said a few things that shouldn't have been said to get my point across and they stopped laughing. They were so mad, but I wasn't worried because what happens in Vegas stays in Vegas. They didn't even look her way when they left because they were hot. I sat next to her and asked why didn't she tell me that she had her period? Then realized I didn't give her a chance to tell me, I just said no. I told her that I would walk her to the nurse's suite. She looked at me like I was crazy and said she had her own pad in her purse. That was fine, but it was way past her just needing a pad. She needed a change of clothes. Something was wrong. I gave her my long sweater and we walked to the nurse's office. I thought why not try to make a connection with her to ease some of her embarrassment, so decided to share my own story. As we walked down the hall, I told her that I know what it's like having a heavy cycle and how it can really mess up your clothes. She didn't say anything. I told her next time to let me know and I would call for Mrs. Woodrow or the other guidance counselor and one of them could walk her to the nurse. She just stared at me and kept walking with a little smirk. I took that blank stare with a hint of a smile as an indication of understanding and confusion.

Chapter Twenty-Five

The Red-hair, Freckled-face Girl

Dear Diary,

Today was a fucked up day. I got my period in class and it went straight through my pants. Worse of all, guess who seen it, yep him. Da boy I been likin' for the last few months. He laughed at me and even got his boy, the one with the mohawk, in on the joke. I wanted to die. I know he ain't eva gonna say nuttin' to me now cause I heard him telling dat boy I was dirty.

I don't know if he told anyone else. I won't know 'til tomorrow at school. I tole Ms. Betty about it when I came in and she said next time just tell the teacher it's an emergency and they would call for the guidance counselor to walk me to the nurses' office. There they go again wit dat nurse bullshit! Why do they want me to go to da nurse all da fuck'n time? I tole her the wet feeling from my period reminded me of him. She nodded her head and tole me to go on with my story.

I began to feel wet again like I had peed on myself, so I thought this time maybe I'd take a shower and went to the bathroom instead. When I took off my shirt, I saw how bright red my chest was. I guess he thought I would have tits like my movah. When I took down my pants and panties I saw blood. I thought I was dying. I grabbed my mom's rob off the hook on the back of the door, put it on, and ran down stairs with my panties in my hand. I was waving my panties in the air when my mother stopped in mid laugh and asked me what in the hell was I doing. I shoved the panties in her face, telling her to look, look!

She pushed my hand out of her face and told whoeva she was talking to she would call 'em back. She hung the phone up with an attitude.

"Who in da hell you think you is putting yo shit in my face, dat shit is nasty," she said angrily. "Are those dem Victoria Secret underwear I bought you last week?"

I looked at her, wondering why she was not trying to help me. Surely I was bleeding to death after what Big Boy did to me and she was mad about some stupid underwear.

"How dare you put ya period drawls in my face?"

"My period," I said. "I got my period. Is this why I

am bleeding?"

"Oh. Okay. Girl, you had me thinking you had lost your mind with dem bloody drawls. Yeah girlie," my mom said clapping. "You becomin' a woman now. Okay, go to da bathroom and look under the sink and get a pad out of the small green bag. I don't think you can handle a tampon yet. Oh, put it in your panties and you'll be straight. If you stomach starts to hurt I'll give you something for dat, to."

She said it like I had done this before, I wanted to ask her questions, but she clapping and singing about me becoming a W-O-M-A-N.

I was just about to go back up da steps when Big Boy walked out of the bedroom scratchin' hisself.

"What's all da noise 'bout, and where da hell you been? A niggah hungry," he said walking up to my mother and kissing her.

I turned my head and began to walk away.

"No wait a minute," my mother said happily ignoring his question. "She got her period today. She is a little lady. Isn't that exciting?"

"Oh yeah, well you could'a kept dat shit to ya self. All dat mean is she can get pregnant if she be messing wit dem little niggahs. I gotta keep an eye out fa that type of shit. Ain't no mo babies coming up in dis camp. We got enough."

"Oh my boo is playin' daddy, ain't dat special?" she said kissing him.

Their kiss got a little to intense for me when I noticed that he was lookin' at me while he was kissin' her and grabbing her butt. I rolled my eyes, turned around, and went upstairs. I couldn't believe that she just tole him I got my period. How embarrassing. Truth is, the bleeding only lasted a little while. When I got my period for real it lasted for 4 days and my stomach did hurt then. I didn't even tell her. Didn't see the point. Ms. Betty asked a few more questions and then let me go.

Anyway, I got a secret dat I can only tell you. Tonight when we was in the shower, I saw that new girl's stuff. She had hair on it, a lot of it. She saw me looking at her and touched it in front of me. I was like OMG! She is a lot older than us so I guess dats why she got so much hair. She looked at me and I smiled and then walked out. I wonder what that is all about. When I find out, you'll be the first to know. Talk to ya lata.

Chapter Twenty-Six

THE BOY

That freckled-face girl got us in trouble. Ms. Brown told us off and said if she found out that we told anybody about it we would spend a lot of time with her after school serving detention. Both them bitches get on my nerves and I knew I wasn't going to detention so for the next 4 days I didn't go to school. I hung out with the man with the purple bag. Unk never knew that I was going to his house some days instead of going to school because I always left at the same time. Anyway, the man with the purple bag said it was too risky to do my "specialty" at my house now because Unk be trippin'. He never explained what he meant about Unk and I never asked.

Nobody was eva at his house, 'cause his mom was a nurse and she worked two shifts. We always had the house to ourselves. I thought it was weird, him staying with his mom with all the money he made. Why didn't he have his own place? I found out later that when prisoners are released they need to have a permanent address. He didn't have any where else to go but to his mom's crib and that probably made his parole officer happy. At least it did for Unk.

Sometimes his boy, the one from up Jessup, would come over and I would do both in the same day making crazy bank. Shiiiit, Kanye West said, "wait 'til I get my money right." My shit was right and my hustle tight.

One day, I was leaving the man with the purple bag house and my Unk was coming up da steps. I almost shit on myself 'cause it was 'round 1 o'clock and school wasn't out yet. My Unk looked at me like he wanted to kill me, grabbed me by my shirt, and dragged me down the steps.

"Ain't you suppose to have ya little ass in school? What da fuck you doin' 'round here?" he yelled at me while dragging me down Fayette Street.

"I was just chillin'," I said trying to keep up 'cause he was draggin' me. I knew Unk was gonna beat my ass when we got back to the house.

"Chillin', huh? Oh, so you big man that don't go to school, huh? Dats why I am getting all dem calls sayn' your child was reported as absent or some shit like dat 'cause you chillin' wit dat niggah?"

I didn't say anything. I couldn't. Shit, I forgot to erase the last message. There was nothing to say. When we got to the house, he threw me into the couch and told me to get butt naked. Dayum, he was gonna beat me with no clothes on? He was mumbling about me hustling like my brother and he wasn't gonna have it, while he waited for me to strip. I felt the tears starting to form in my eyes. He looked at me like my tears weren't fazing him and paced the floor.

"Dem fuck'n tears don't mean nuttin' to me home boy, get dem fuck'n clothes off."

Unk was from the old school. He used to tell me stories about how him and Ma would get beatings butt naked by Grandma when they got in trouble. Momma learned quicker than he did and stopped getting beatings early. My Unk didn't learn that quickly. He told me grandma's beating weren't worse than jail time and he wish he had learned from her.

I stood there naked and he grabbed me by the arm and swung the belt. I thought I was gonna faint. He swung it again and began to tell me how I shouldn't skip school and hang with hustlas. How I won't be a hustla like my brother. Not on his watch. Mercifully, his cell phone rang. He stopped beating me long enough to answer it. Unk listened to whoever was on the telephone. I stood there with tears in my eyes, too scared to move and too scared to pick up my pants. After he hung up, he told whoeva was on the telephone that he would be right down.

"Put ya fuck'n clothes on and don't you leave this house. I gotta go get ya brother," he said and walked out the door.

He's got to go get my brother. Oh shit. He must be in trouble. Shoot, I am glad my hustle ain't like dat. It's just us, no police and no guns, and I make all the money I want. I picked up my shirt, put my pants back on, and went upstairs to my room. I sat on the bed and took the money out of my pants pocket and began to count it. Dayum, I made $260 in an hour. Shit, bet my brother ain't making money like this that quick. I laid back on the bed and noticed my thang. Shit, it was hard? Counting my money got me hard. So I did what I do for my customers and fell asleep.

I woke up to the sound of my Unk's voice yelling at someone.

"You lucky they let you go, 'cause they could'a left ya ass in baby bookings," Unk screamed. He was mad as shit.

"I ain't need you to come and scoop me. My boys was comin'," my brother yelled.

"Oh yeah, you'se a dumb niggah. You been sittin' down there for 8 hours and ain't none of them niggahs come and scooped you yet."

"What eva man, dems my peoples. They was comin'."

"Shut the fuck up. Ya sound stupid. Them niggahs ain't thinkin' bout you. You only make them small change. Niggah, don't you know you replaceable?"

I put my shirt on, zipped up my pants, and ran downstairs and there was Unk and my brother arguing. My Unk looked up at me and shook his head.

"Oh and here comes the other dumb fuck. Skippin' school to hang with the older niggahs, tryin' to hustle like ya brother. Y'all is some dumb motha fuckas. Don't you get it? Ain't nothing hot 'bout dem streets. You'd think wit ya momma being sick you lil' niggahs would ack like ya got some sense."

"Don't say shit bout my momma," said my brother moving closer to him.

"She laying up in da hospice dying and you out here actin' like wanna be ganstas wit ya punk asses."

"Say one mo thing 'bout my momma and I'ma—..."

"You gonna what? Huh niggah? Oh so yo da big man of da house? Dats ya beef with me? You stepping to me, son?" Unk said punching his own chest. "Don't get it twisted. I will fuck you up. I ain't no punk."

My brother laughed, "Niggah you'se clown. Coming out tryin' to be betta than other people. You'se joke. It ain't nuttin' to me to drop you were you stand," my brother said now standing in Unk's face.

I came down to the bottom of the steps when my Unk looked at me and I stopped in my tracks.

"Do it," Unk said breathing hard and standing in my brother's face.

My brother raised his fist and before it landed Unk had knocked him down. He was wailing on my brother, but my brother was throwing blows, too. They were fighting like enemies. My Unk slammed him on the coffee table and then began to kick and stomp him. My brother was laying on the now broken table screaming when I ran over to Unk and tried to get him to stop. He pushed me into the wall and I hit my head. My brother got up screaming don't touch my brother and hit Unk from behind and they went at it again. I sat there on the floor holding my head when I heard sirens. My Unk stopped hitting my brother and moved away from him.

"I ain't going back to jail fa ya punk ass," he said as he walked into the kitchen. My brother was broke down but managed to get up. He walked right past me and left. All of a sudden the police where pounding on the door.

Chapter Twenty-Seven

Ms. Wilson

"Brownie, I need to vent," Willie said, coming into my room and sitting at my desk and chair I kept near my desk for the many private conversations that came along with the job. "You know he hasn't been here for over a week and nobody knows where he is."

"Willie, who are you talking about? Your favorite or your man? Because for a second it sounded like you were talking about Calvin." I knew she thought the boy was special, even if he had no idea that he was. She understood his pain because they both shared the bond of having an ill mom during their middle-school years. She had lost her mom and he was about to lose his.

"Girl, I may have had something to do with that. I had to get on him and his little mohawk buddy about picking on another student," I said putting books away from today's lesson.

"Huh? Something happened between you two?" she inquired rolling her eyes. She knew I had a mouth on me when it came to discipline. "You didn't tell me about that. What happened?"

"You know the little red-hair, freckled-face girl in my Reading class?

The one who lives in the group home, real quiet?"

"Yeah I know her; you can't miss her in this school. Isn't she like one of four white students in the building?"

"Um hum, you can see her miles away with that bright red hair. I tell you she is one little girl with problems that I would never had dreamed of." I thought about telling Willie about the meeting we had and the information that was shared, but figured it wasn't the right time. She was already upset about her favorite student.

"Well, she got her period in class and it leaked through her clothes. Of course she tried to conceal it, but your little darling saw it and made a small mockery of her with his friend. I took both of them in the corner and told them something that ended with detention. Girl, he was mad at me. I know I was every kind of bitch in the world, but he didn't say anything to me about it. At least he had enough sense not to. He hasn't been to school since that day."

"Oh Lord, Brownie. God only knows what came between 'get over here' and 'detention'," she said smiling.

I just smiled at her and said Vegas baby, Vegas. Some of the kids call me the spirit crusher, because I don't take no mess. Some people may think that is a bad name, but I wear it like a badge of honor. Funny how they would give me such a name when they would tell me they love me or wonder where I am when I'm out. My students know excuses are not accepted and their best is the only thing they better bring. Slacking is not an option and when they slack I will tell them the truth, regardless of how they may feel before or after my comments. I know when they have tried and I know when they have thrown something together at the last minute. Our kids deserve the truth, because the world is hard and swallowing people whole is what it does best. My kids know that in this room we are in the business of learning and Brownie is a hard boss, so you better bring your A-game if you want to get paid.

"Well it could be that, but I told you his mom is now in hospice?"

"Yes, you did. Have you heard anything from Mrs. Woodrow about that?"

"No, but she did tell me that the Pupil Personnel Worker (PPW) was going to their house to find out why he has been absent before they take it to court. I am wondering if I should go by his house this week, to see for myself."

"You're going to do a home visit, Willie?" I couldn't help but laugh because she was always going to somebody's house. "Want me to ride shot gun and bring one, too," I asked laughing.

"Shut up Brownie, I am serious. His mother is not going to live long if she is there and he needs somebody."

"What about his uncle? Isn't he taking care of him?"

"The uncle, who just got out of jail, uncle? If he was, why isn't he in school," she asked with the attitude of a concerned parent.

I didn't say anything because she had a point. "Alright Willie, when do you want to go? You drive, wear your superwoman cape, and I will bring the shot gun," I said with a smile. She looked at me and smiled, but it wasn't real. She was really concerned about him and scared of what we may find out.

CHAPTER TWENTY-EIGHT

The Red-hair, Freckled-face Girl

Dear Diary,

School hasn't been that bad lately. I just knew dat boy I liked and his mohawk friend was gonna come to school and tell everybody about my period coming through my pants. I was ready for the jokes and had even came up with a few names that I thought they was gonna call me, but nope. He didn't even come to school for like a week. Ms. Brown asked the Boy with the Mohawk if he was sick or did he know why he wasn't coming. His boy didn't know. He hadn't talked to 'em. I heard Ms. Wilson was asking in her class, to. All I know is that he wasn't there and that was fine wit me.

At lunch I heard some people talkin' bout there was a shooting at his house 'cause they saw the police there one night. Another girl said that he was moving 'cause his mom was sick or dead or something. But the one dat had everybody trippin' was what this one girl had said in health class. Mr. King was talking to us about sex and homosexuality and this one boy was like Mr. King I got a question. Mr. King warned 'em to watch his words before he spoke and that they could get you in trouble or sumthing like dat. The boy asked what if you give a hand job or if you be givin' brain to a dude, does that mean you is a faggy? All the kids bust out laughing, me to. Mr. King didn't even look like he thought it was funny. He told us that type of question was not appropriate for school. Anyway, he didn't answer the question. Then out of nowhere somebody said we gotta faggy in our class, and people started giggling. Mr. King went off. I don't remember what he said because I was listenin' to the girl behind me saying dat she heard that the boy I like be hanging out wit dis dude who just got out of jail. She heard that he be giving him head and hand jobs. ILLLLL and he called ME nasty? Can you believe it? They say'n he a faggy. He suppose to be havin' sex with 'em to, but I don't know. He to cute to be a faggy. I hope he ain't.

CHAPTER TWENTY-NINE

THE BOY

I went to visit Momma today with Unk. She didn't look like Momma. She was all skinny and frail with tubes coming out from her arm. I sat by her bed while she slept while Unk went to talk to her doctors. I hadn't seen my brother since the night of the fight. My Unk never said any more about it again. I wondered if my brother had even seen Momma since she been up here.

The night of the fight was so crazy. I had never seen people get down like that before. I mean, I seen two crack heads fight, but they was pushing and wrestling more than anything else. Unk and my brother were throwing blows. I had a lump on the back of my head from when I fell and hit the wall. Somebody had called the po-po because they were banging on the door like crazy. My Unk handled the police cool as shit. They banged on the door like they were 'bout to knock the fucker down. He straightened his clothes, took a deep breath, and opened the door. Two officers stood at the door, one big and bald and the other tall with twists in his head. Unk stood in the door so they couldn't really see in the house.

"Ah, good evening sir we are here because someone called about a disturbance," said the big bald one with the bushy mustache, while turning down his radio.

"Nah sir, no real disturbance, just a little family stuff," Unk said real cool.

"Well is everyone alright, may we come in?" asked the tall one with the twist.

"Everything is cool now," said Unk, moving around because the tall officer was trying to see in the house.

"Well the table in there seems to be broken. Are you sure everything is okay?" asked the tall one frowning at Unk.

All I could think of was what if they come in and see me on the floor holding my head, they gonna think Unk did something to me. I didn't know if I should move or what. So I just slide over into the kitchen real quiet.

Unk breathed in real hard and said, "Look here officer, my nephews had a fight and the table was broken while they tussled."

"Where are the boys now sir?" asked the short bald one.

"My youngest nephew is upstairs and the older one ran out. See their momma real sick and it is starting to get to 'em," Unk said real believable like.

For a second I almost forgot about the fight between Unk and my brother and thought dayum that shit sound true.

"Well we would like to see the younger one," said the bald one. "Just to be sure."

"Um, off-i-sah, that's really not necessary, he been through enough tonight, everything is cool now."

"Well if everything is *cool now* like you say it is then it will only take a minute," said the tall one reaching for something.

You can tell by the way Unk spoke that these niggah's was getting on his nerves. "Aight den. I ain't got no problem with dat, Off-i-sah. No problem at all."

My Unk called for me and I came to the door. The officers asked me what happened and Unk looked at me with wide eyes, but he played it cool.

"Me and my brother had a fight," I said looking at the floor.

"About what?" asked the tall officer.

"Go in da house. You answered his question," Unk said looking at the tall officer.

I didn't move because I didn't know what to do. Unk turned and looked me in my eyes, and leaned his head in the direction of the house. I went in, and the tall officer said, "he didn't answer my question."

"Oh, but he did Off-i-sah. You wanted to know if he had a fight. He told you he did. The fight has been squashed and we cool. Thank you for coming by, 'ppreciate it," Unk said. He stepped back in the house and closed the door. You could hear the tall officer saying something about fuck des niggahs, I oughta knock da door down. The short bald one told him lets go and they must have walked down our steps. It was quiet for a sec, then you heard a thump on the door. I jumped, Unk didn't, he said "dat bitch ass cop probably threw sumthing or kicked da door." Unk locked the door and went upstairs like nothing happened.

CHAPTER THIRTY

The Red-hair, Freckled-face Girl

Dear Diary,

OMG, guess what happened? Remember I told you 'bout the older girl who just got here? The one who showed me her stuff and felt it while lookin' at me in da shower?...Well she sat down with me at dinner and we talked. She is 16 and goes to Woodhills High. I wish she went to school wit me. I would have had fun with her. She had been in Meadowlands, all the bad kids go der, before she came here.

She asked me why was I in here and I told her I was beefin' wit my mom and she just nodded. She said she had beat up her movah for not letting her friend stay over. Dayum, can you believe dat? She beat up her own movah! Dat shit is crazy. Maybe I should have her beat down Big Boy and I can move back home.

Anyway, she sat there talking to me and everybody was watchin' us, even Ms. Betty. She didn't look to happy, but so what, I like her. She's cool. She wanted to know what we do for fun 'round here and I was telling her about game night and skating. She said game night sounded boring as fuck, but skating at Roll n Skate (we called it Shake n Shoot) would be fun. I tole her about how we go to da mall every other Saturday, she said she don't shop, but she lift and laughed. She asked me was they going to the mall this weekend and we was. She said I could hang with her if I wanted to. If not, she would see me back here. I was gonna hang wit her. She looked at me funny, kinda like da way Big Boy use to look at me and tole me she would see me later, she wanted to watch American Idol and left the table. She left her plate and stuff, but I didn't care I put 'em in da sink for her. She is mad cool. Mad cool.

CHAPTER THIRTY-ONE

Ms. Brown

You know what I've noticed about middle school kids?" I asked Willie while we were grading papers. "Middle school students don't smile. They always look depressed."

"Humph," Willie said thinking about my statement.

"Think about it. When they come into school in the morning they look mad. When you say good morning, they grumble it back or ignore you all together. They never come in cheery or leave cheery if you really think about it. They don't smile, only laugh when they are talking about someone else to make them feel bad. Have you ever seen a happy middle school kid?"

"Wow, when you think about it, some of them are only happy when they are getting something or if they have a good report card. They never really just smile for the sake of smiling. Maybe it's because they like watching movies that are melancholy, blood filled with someone getting shot, or dying."

"Don't forget there are no peaceful deaths just horrible ones."

"Were we like that? I mean, we had Jason and Freddy Cougar, but we had fun movies, happy silly satirical movies, like Star Wars, and E.T., and Breakin'," I said pop locking.

"You are a fool," Willie said laughing. "I guess it's because of the times we live in. The music, the reality TV shows, the internet, the glamorized thug life, video vixens, and the illegal ways to get paid would warp any developing mind."

"Oh, please don't forget the news. They only show the positive information after the damn weather. No one watches the news after the weather. It's too late. You have already heard about who got killed, the economy, terrorist, you can't eat this, the messed up school system, and now your weather. Your mind is already tainted. The news could really mess up an adult's mind, if they aren't careful."

"Yep, sex is everywhere. It's not even seen as beautiful or soulfully orgasmic with the right person," Willie said, with her eyes closed.

"Would you like to be alone? You're thinking about somebody and I feel like I am interrupting," I cut her a meaningful look.

"Girl, flashback. Anyway, we can't compete with all of that."

"I can't compete with what just happened to you. Girl, get it together until you get home."

"I am good, but see, our children will never know that sex is supposed to be full of love and not just you getting caught in the bathroom bent over the toilet screwing some boy so he has an orgasm."

"Oh, I remember that episode. I can't recall her name, but she was a brick house. Doing it in the bathroom and got caught with that funny looking boy. You know she didn't even feel bad about it? She said she was like a video vixen, but in school."

"Like I said, we can't compete. You know who I really feel sorry for are the men who try to come and teach. These boys are not trying to hear what a man has to say. There is no male figure in the house, and here comes this male teacher trying to pull rank for 45 minutes. That's a struggle within itself."

"Makes you wonder why more men aren't teachers."

"I hate to sound like the stereotypical statistics, but they are either in jail, dead, hustling, or don't care about giving back to the community. Some men are too busy making money in corporate America. A teacher doesn't make a substantial amount of money until they reach the administrative track. With that comes all of the politics and money games to boot. Teaching is not an appealing profession, so you can't really blame them for not wanting to teach."

Chapter Thirty-Two

The Boy

I didn't want to go back to see Momma again. I couldn't deal with it. She didn't even know I was there. Unk said he didn't want to lie to me, but the doctors told him that she wouldn't make it through the week. I just looked at him. I kept asking him was he sure and he just hugged me. We both cried while standing in Momma's room. She was leaving me. I couldn't breathe so the nurse took me out and talked to me. She helped me to calm down. I didn't go back.

While I was in there I told her I loved her and that I would do good in school. I would make her proud of me. I wanted her to say something, anything, but she just slept.

The last time I heard Momma's voice was when she was singing when she was high on that shit my brother gave her. I didn't know if he even came here to see about her. Did he even know that she was gonna die any day now? Not later, but real fuck'n soon? We weren't gonna have any parents.

My brother's dad was killed in a drive by when he was like 3 years old. My momma met my father when he was like 5 and then she had me. My father is locked up for life for shooting a cop. At first, he was on death row, but then this black lawyer got it to life with no parole. I didn't go see him. He told Momma during one of her visits to never bring me up there. He didn't want me to see him like that. Besides he wouldn't be able to do his bid if he ever had a face to go with my name—his name. She never took me and I never asked to go.

I use to go see my grandma sometimes, but when she got sick that stopped. That's the only funeral I ever went to. My momma said my dad was trying to get out to go to the funeral, but I didn't see him. At least I don't think I did. Now, Momma is gonna die and I ain't gonna have nobody. I don't know if Unk is gonna wanna take care of me after she dies. He ain't got no kids so he can leave if he wants to. Dayum, this is fucked up.

CHAPTER THIRTY-THREE

The Red-hair, Freckled-face Girl

Dear Diary,

Gotta tell you 'bout today. It was off da hook. Ms. Betty took us to Security Mall today for our weekend outing. We were allowed to walk around, but we had to go with a partner. I told Ms. Betty I was going with the new girl, but she said she didn't like dat idea. I asked her why and she tole me some shit like she is older and may have different interests. I begged and begged and tole her I would be good. Ms. Betty agreed, but she tagged along wit us. She didn't walk right next to us, but she was close behind. The new girl called Ms. Betty the group home po-po. I felt like it was my fault dat she was following us around. The new girl said dat bitch ain't bother her, that she been locked up befoe. I was amazed. I wanted to know why she was locked up and how long, but she nevah bought it back up and I was to scared to ask.

We went in Old Navy and was looking at some shirts and pants. Ms. Betty looked around too, but she wasn't up on us anymore. The new girl said she was gonna go try on the pants and said for me to get some stuff and try it on, to. We went to the dressing room and the new girl went to the one all da way in the back. I followed her 'cause I was about to go in the one next to her, but she tole me we could share. I was like ok. It was tight, but she didn't seem to mind. She took off her shirt and she had the biggest titi's I had eva seen. She didn't' have on no bra. I stared at 'em and she didn't seem to mind. She tried on three shirts and decided on the one she wanted. It was $25. We only had $20. I didn't know how she was gonna get da shirt 'cause she didn't have enough money. She tole me to watch dis. She took out a small piece of aluminum foil wrapped it around the security tag thing, put the shirt back on under her shirt, and walked out da store. I was scared as shit. She walked right out dat store. She smiled at me and then we went into another store with Ms. Betty right behind us. She didn't even know. I was pumped. We went into Foot Locker and she was trying on a pair of shorts. She went into the dressing room and did the same thang. I watched her change. She took her pants off and I looked right at her stuff. I couldn't help it. She saw me looking at her, pulled her panties to the side, and touched it again. This time I watched. My face was all red, but I watched. She put her finger in it and licked it. She was putting her finger in my face, when Ms. Betty asked are we alright in there. We both answered yes and bust out laughing. She put her pants on over the shorts and we walked right out the door. Nobody knew nuttin'. We went to da food court to get something to take back to the home and that was it. I can't believe she got a whole fuck'n outfit for free. She didn't get caught or nuttin'. Next time she said I could do it, to. I can't wait.

CHAPTER THIRTY-FOUR

Ms. Wilson

Another week has gone by and he still hadn't been to school. The PPW had gone by and he said no one answered the door. He told Mrs. Woodrow that he would try again and then file the paperwork for court. I was nervous now. It had been damn near 2 weeks and no one had heard from or seen him. I heard some of the kids talking about him hanging with some older man who just got out of jail, but I thought maybe the older man was the uncle. I knew he had served time and had come to take care of the two boys, but I don't believe he is doing such a good job. So damn it, I am going today after school to see about him. I know Brownie said she would go with me, but I don't want him to feel uncomfortable with her coming to his house. Especially since they did have words, if you will. He may clam up and not talk to me if she is there. I'm sure she is concerned about him, but I think she is more concerned about me. She told me that the stress was showing in my face and that she wanted us to go and have a spa day to help release some of the tension. And besides, she said she was sexually backed up. She is so crazy. She always knows how to make me laugh even if it is TMI or just plain nasty. I know I told her Thursday, but there is nothing wrong with the present. Matter of fact, I won't even tell her that I'm going. I will just go and call her later.

The last 10 minutes of class seemed to go so slow. When the bell finally did ring the kids and I were scrambling to get out of the door. My bag was packed and all I had to get was my purse out of the closet and go. I had the address in my pocket and my car keys in hand. I felt funny taking the back stairs to my car. Why in the hell was I sneaking? Damn it, I'm grown. I knew Brownie would try to go with me if she saw me, so I had to do it this way. I got in my car and sped off before I got trapped by the waiting school buses. He should be home because he wasn't in school. I won't stay long, just long enough to ask him how he's doing, let him know he is missed, and that he needs to get to school before the PPW comes back. I found a parking spot right in front of the address that I had written down on the paper. Why am I so nervous? It's not like I have never done a home visit before. I got out of my car, hit the alarm, and walked up his steps. I knocked on the door. No answer. I knocked on the door again and this time a man came to the door. His eyes were blood shot red and he smelled like something. This is probably the uncle who is taking care of him. Is he drunk? No wonder the boy isn't coming to school. No one is here to make him go.

"May I help you?" he asked with both a sour breath and attitude.

"Ah yes, I am Ms. Wilson, from Harlem Ridge City school and I am here to check on…"

"I was just about to call the school and let you know," he said with a shaky voice.

My heart stopped. Let me know… Let me know what? "Oh, I was

concerned about..."

"Yes, ma'am. See his mother has been ill and in hospice for the last few weeks and um, um she passed this morning."

"Oh, she passed this morning? I am so sorry for your loss."

"Thank you. We knew it was coming, but you're nevah really prepared for death. Ya know what I mean?"

"Oh, of course. How is he? Is there anything I can do? We have a pretty good relationship. He would talk about his mom all the time. Is he okay?"

"He is hurting bad right now. But that is expected. We are all hurting," he said with a sniffle.

"How is his brother?" I asked not caring if I was being too nosey or not.

"We haven't seen him in a few weeks. He doesn't know yet. Some friends of mine are out looking for him to bring him here so we can tell'em," he said looking down.

"Jesus," was all I could say. "Can I see him? Would that be alright?"

"Sure, come in. I'll ask 'im."

I walked into the modestly furnished row home. It was clean and seemed well kept. Damn, and I was thinking the house would be roach infested with cigarette buds and Crown Chicken cartons all over the place. Am I that bourgeoisie? Of course he may have smelled, he was hurting and probably had a drink. Willie, that is so trifling of you… You tell your students all the time not to prejudge and then you just did to the *Nth* power. I jumped when he came back.

"Um ma'am. I'm sorry, what is your name again?"

"Ms. Wilson. Sanaye Wilson," I said extending my hand for a handshake. Something I should have done after he answered the door. He shook it very gently and held it for a while. I understood.

When he let go he said, "Ms. Wilson, he said he wasn't ready to see you yet, but he hopes you will come to the funeral."

My heart stopped as I nodded yes. "Tell him I will be there. Um, if you have a pen and paper, I will give you my number." He picked up a pad and pen off the chair by the door and flipped the page. I noticed a list of something, maybe funeral arrangements. I gave him my cell and home numbers and told him to call me if he needed any assistance from me or the school. I also told him to let his nephew know that he can call me anytime if he wanted to talk to me. Right now, who gave a shit about the school system and how they may view this? This boy needed me and I was going to be there. I gave my condolences again and he walked me to the door. He thanked me and even watched me until I got in my car safely. When the door was closed, I locked my door and put my head down on the staring wheel and cried. I cried hard. I cried for him, a young man living in Baltimore city with no mother or father. I cried for a boy whose soul was shattered and may never be repaired. I cried for him and me. I cried for mothers who had to leave their children alone before they're grown. I cried for me, because it was like losing my mother all over again.

CHAPTER THIRTY-FIVE

MS. BROWN

When I look at the children in my school I sometimes prejudge them based on their appearance and what I think is the appropriate future for them. In the Bible, Matthew 7:1 reads, *Judge not, that you be not judged* and Proverbs 18:21 reads, *Life and death are in the power of the tongue.* These scriptures are no longer applicable to my life since my experience of misfortunate events, teaching being one of them. Therefore, I am exempt. It's funny how I can look at a child and see their future, yet I can barely see my own. I see that this boy is going to jail; that one will go on to college; he will play basketball or work in corporate America; oh and that girl will end up pregnant before tenth grade; this one will make it; and she will work in a medical office; or she will be a stripper. It's written all over her and her momma gave her the name already. Who am I to put them in the category of who will and who won't make it? The drug dealers, the club hoppers, the churchgoers, the weed smokers, the hard workers, and the dream makers are all deciphered by their faces and attitudes. My thoughts, my beliefs, and my low expectations for the next generation… built on the foundation of my own issue. It's like playing I-Spy with no crystal ball, but just that feeling in the pit of your stomach.

I don't know how I became this way. Maybe I judge because I was never one of the popular girls in middle or high school. It seemed like all of the other kids judged me based on my clothes, hair, and looks. Judged? Nah, I was picked on. I was bullied through much of my academic career until college. I never thought I was beautiful because of the freckles on my nose and the short hair, when everyone else's' hair was long. I was different... awkwardly tall in the eighth grade with no curves at all. My height made me look like I was 16 when I was only 12 in middle school. I talked to guys who were 18 to 23 years old when I was in the seventh grade. I was hot in the pants because I liked the attention. I thought that made me special. Well, at least in my mind it did.

The girls I teach now think they have lying down pat; huh, I was a liar extraordinaire. I should have received an Oscar for best actress when I was around men who were older than me. So, I do understand the temptation my female students endure. Until your appetite for attention has been quenched, you will always go back to the well of older men to satisfy your thirst. It's like a junkie chasing their first high, knowing they will never attain it again. I still prefer older men now. I guess my thirst has yet to be satisfied. Is this a manifestation of my own pain? There is never a good day of the week for pain, no matter how old or young. Pain is a bitch and she takes no prisoners. She rides shotgun with me every day. When I look at myself in the mirror, I see pain more than I see myself. She changes her hair like women with weaves. Sometimes she wears depression, other days its self-pity, and on the weekend she pulls out envy and anger. Other days, I don't know who I see. The girl who was abused and became promiscuous because of the desire to be touched again or the woman who would sleep with men to find a love; yet, has never found it. Why? My daddy loved me, didn't he? Sure he did. I grew up in a house with both parents and I am *still* messed up. You can't blame those little girls without fathers for their behavior, right? No wonder the girl with the red hair is so messed up. She is in pain. Her mother chose a man over her safety. I would be angry and full of vengeance, too. Pain is pain, be it death, destruction of a relationship, or family. It's still a bitch! The only difference between the red-hair, freckled-face girl and me is that I am better at hiding it... At least now I am.

CHAPTER THIRTY-SIX

Ms. WILSON

The service was one of the saddest I had been to. His mother laid in a pretty coffin—if coffins can be pretty—in a beautiful white dress. To me, she didn't look like the woman I met 2 years ago at a Parent-Teacher conference. Her body was small and frail; her petite hands in white gloves as they rested on her stomach. I couldn't handle this. It was too much. Some of the kids from the school were there with their parents. Mrs. Harris and Mrs. Woodrow tended to the students who were having difficulty. Brownie was there for me. I took this harder than I had expected. She wasn't my mother, but she was somebody's mother. We stood there for a while and all I could think about was my mom.

I remembered standing there with my father and my two sisters looking at my mother for the last time. She looked small and her cheeks weren't as full, but she was Mommy. I laid my head on her chest and cried. I wanted her to get up and come home with us, but she was cold. Her hands—cold and stiff. I kissed her cheek. It was cold. The warmth had left her body for good. She was cold. I would no longer hear her songs of laughter or be silenced by her hugs when I cried. She would no longer leave faint lip impressions on my skin when she would kiss me before bed. She was cold. My father cried while my sister, Casey, tried to comfort him—stepping into our mother's shoes right there in front of her coffin. We stood there for what seemed liked forever just trying to soak up every memory of her before they closed the casket. I didn't want to forget what she looked like, the sound of her voice, her smell, all of the things that made her my mom because once the casket was closed I would never see her again. I was so scared that I would forget. I had to remember. Needed to remember. My mom.

"Willie, let's sit down sweetie, the family is about to come in," said Brownie, taking my hand and leading me back to our seats. I wiped my face and tried to compose myself for him. He had asked for me to be there, and I was. I needed to be strong for him; my tears could fall in the morning.

He was looking around the church, in search of something. I could tell he was looking for me. When he came closer to the front of the church, he saw me sitting with Brownie a few rows in the back from where the family would sit. He just kept staring at me, so I continued to smile at him. I tried to mouth to him that I am here if he needs me when his brother let out a yell.

"MOMMMA! NO Momma, Momma, Momma..."

The scream his brother let out scared Brownie and I because we both jumped. I didn't expect it because his brother was always the tough one and he lost it. No matter how tough he is, he is still a child. His scream caused a domino effect because the uncle had just slumped over, too. Lord, he is walking alone.

"Brownie, I gotta go to him," I said as I let go of her hand and jumped out of the pew.

He was standing still in the middle of the aisle watching his brother lay on their mother crying and yelling for her to wake up. He was trembling when I put my arm around him.

"If you don't want to go up, you don't have to," I said. He shook his head yes and we walked to the casket. His breathing got harder and he was holding my hand so tight. One of the ushers helped his brother and uncle to their seats and we stood in front of the casket.

"Doesn't she look beautiful?" he whispered.

"Absolutely, beautiful," I said. His tears were silent, but hard. He didn't make noise. He just said Mommy I love you, kissed her, and stared. We stood for a while and it seemed like everything went silent. I stood there with him until they began the service. I was sure he was thinking what I thought about when my own mom passed. This is the last time I will see her, so let me look so I can remember.

CHAPTER THIRTY-SEVEN

The Red-hair, Freckled-face Girl

Dear Diary,

School was sad today. I found out that the boy that I like movah died. Ms. Brown thought that it would be nice if we made him cards. I made one with his favorite colors, red and black. I know he is sad. Some of the kids in our class went to the funeral and brought back programs. His movah was pretty. She had long hair and funny looking eyes. Some of da kids said she didn't look the same at the funeral because she was sick, but they said she had on a really pretty white dress. This girl said Ms. Wilson went to and she cried. I didn't know she knew his movah like dat. Anyway, he is suppose to come back to school next week, so we shall see how he really is.

Ok, enough of dat sad shit, let me tell you 'bout this girl. She is so sweet and fun. She eats dinner wit me sometimes and lets me come into her room. But, tonight was off da chain. First, she was showing me how to take aluminum foil from the kitchen without getting caught. After dat, she showed me how to wrap it around the security tags so when we go out to da mall this Saturday I won't get caught. Then we was just chill'n listenin' to music when she asked me if I eva kissed a girl befoe? I hadn't, just my mom and I wasn't sure if she counted or not. She was like nah not ya moms, but someone like me. I tole her no 'cause I hadn't. She was like cool, so you'se a virgin, right? I didn't know. Big Boy had done it to me and I was bleeding and stuff so I guess I wasn't. I told her about what Big Boy had did and she got so mad. She tole me if she had been around she would'a fucked 'em up. She tole me from now on she would be my protector. I was glad. She came over to where I was and gave me a hug. She held me for a long time and when we finally let go she stared at me. I was smiling and staring back at her to. Then she kissed me. She kissed me. Can you believe it? She put her tongue in my mouth and her tongue wiggled around real fast. I had nevah been tongue kissed befoe', specially not by no girl. Her spit tasted like strawberries and I liked that taste. I moved my tongue like she did, shit I didn't know how to tongue kiss. She made a moan and she grabbed my butt. I swallowed her spit when I tried to breath and started choking. It was so funny 'cause she was pounding my back hard as shit. She asked me was I aight and we laughed. She gave me another kiss, and tole me good night. Guess that was my signal to leave. I got up and she said lata Redz. Yep she called me Redz. Dats my nickname for her only.

Redz, dats me.

CHAPTER THIRTY-EIGHT

THE BOY

I wasn't ready to go back to school, but Unk said I had to go. He let me stay out a week after Ma's funeral, just so I could get my head together. I hadn't seen my brother since the day of the funeral and was wondering where he could be. I wasn't sure who was gonna take care of me now that Moms was gone and my brother was nowhere to be found. The morning I was going back to school I asked Unk was he leaving me?

"Hell nah, I ain't leavin' you boy. I made a promise to ya momma and mysef dat I would be here to take care of you so you could be betta dan me. Know what I'm sayin'?" Unk said smiling and nodding his head. "Word, I luv you lil' man and I'ma try my best to protect, provide, and take care of ya. You got my word, son. Come 'er and show me some love."

He hugged me and I felt safe. He told me he wasn't leaving and I was happy. I wish my brother was here and we could be a real family, but for now I'm happy for Unk.

"Aight lil' man, school time," he said handing me my book bag. "We gots to get movin'."

He said "we". That made me smile. Unk walked me to school my first few days back. It was aight, but weird 'cause most of da time the walk was quiet. He didn't say much and neither did I. He was just there. He didn't walk me into the building or nothing like dat, but he did walk me to the parking lot.

"Aight lil' man, see ya afta school," he said giving me dap.

"Okay, Unk," I said and headed to the eighth-grade doors. Some of the kids who were walking by said hi, told me to stay up, and then some kids giggled. I heard them whispering about me being back and asking who was that guy walking me to school. I didn't really care about why they was laughing—fuck 'em. I went into the building looking around like it was my first day again. I went to my locker, but couldn't remember the combination so I went to ask Mr. Mack. Mr. Mack was my homeroom and Math teacher. He reminded me of Unk because he was tall and skinny like 'em. He smiled, gave me dap, and told me he was sorry to hear about my mom. He got me my locker combo and told me to make it quick because we were starting the review of the new unit. See Mr. Mack was cool. He would give us candy when we did well on a test or when our work on the board was correct. But, Mr. Mack wasn't the one to fuck wit either. He would take out his phone and call ya house with the quickness and then to make it worse, put you on the phone to talk to 'em. He made math fun and I liked that. I put my stuff in my locker, went back in, and got to work.

I felt weird being back in Ms. Brown's class because the last time I was here she was telling me off. I was a little worried about what she would say when I came in, but Ms. Brown always tells us that once a beef is squashed then it stays squashed. I was surprised to see how Ms. Brown had the other students make me cards saying how sorry they were about my mom or to keep my head up. Even my Boy with the Mohawk made me a card, but for some reason didn't want to sit with me. That's cool, he probably didn't know what to say.

What really caught me off guard was the card from the red-hair, freckled-face girl. Hers was the best because she had my favorite colors on it. How did she know? I don't know, but it was nice. I thanked her and apologized for making fun of her. She looked at me with her mouth open like I was crazy, but said thanks and went back to her work.

Ms. Wilson had brought me lunch my first day back from Chic-fil-a. I ate with her and she asked me how things were going and if I had seen my brother. I told her that he seemed to have taken it harder than anyone else. When we went to bury our mom, he dayum near jumped in with her. Kept crying and saying he didn't want her to leave. He wasn't doing well at all. My Unk tried to comfort him, but he wasn't doing so good himself. At the house, my brother kept talking to himself about how he was just trying to help. Me and Unk was the only ones who knew what he was talking about.

"What did he mean, he was only trying to help?" asked Ms. Wilson.

"I can't say, but he was always trying to make her feel betta." I left that topic alone. I think she knew what I meant. She nodded her head and took a bite of her sandwich.

But anyway, I told her there was this chick there that I didn't know. She hung around my brother all day. I guess she was his girl or something because she kept rubbing his back, getting him food, and stuff. Shit, he wasn't paying her no mine. It wasn't too many people at the house, but some of them were my mom's friends, people from the neighborhood, and my Unk's peeps—the man with the purple bag and the other dude from the basement. I didn't see any of my brother's boys. I just saw the girl.

During lunch, Ms. Wilson offered me help catching up on my work. She said she would stay after school with me until we got it all done. I was glad she was around to help. For the next couple of days I stayed by myself. I didn't feel like messing with anybody. I ate lunch with Ms. Wilson another day and then the day after that I ate by myself. I guess I was learning to deal with not having my mom around.

I hadn't seen the man with the purple bag since the funeral until one day I was walking home from school and I saw him on somebody's steps. He came down the steps, asked me where I was going, and started to walk with me. He smelled, but he always smelled. While we walked, he wanted to know if I was up to doing my "specialty" and told me that he gave me time to get my head right since my moms had passed.

"A hustla can't stay out da game for too long. His customers need da product. Either they get it from you or the next niggah," he said while he walked with me down the street. "So what's da deal Lil' Shorty? If you ain't up for no specialty den I will take a #1," he said smiling, sucking his teeth.

He made it sound like he was at McDonalds. I was down to give him the #1 as he put it because today at school this kid had on a pair of the new Lebron James and I wanted a pair, too. I told him I would meet him at his crib tomorrow after school.

"Afta school? Shit. I gotta wait all day for something I can do myself? Nah, den. Shit, if I gotta wait 'til afta school, I might as well get da specialty. I ain't wait'n all day for a hand job," he said mad. "Memba, you gotta keep ya hustle tight. You don't want to lose ya customer," he said, but to me it sounded like a question.

Lose my customers? Nah, I don't wanna lose any customers, but who in the hell would want this hustle besides some faggy dude or some crack hoe? I wasn't either one of those. I stayed clean and I did a good job. Did he forget how tight my skills are?

I wonder if Momma had gotten better would she had become one of the women that do shit for chocolate city. Was she better off dead or would she had gotten better and became a hoe on the street? Would my brother keep her high or turn her out and make her do shit to his boys?

"Hey, you listening to me? Look, so what up Lil' Shorty? Do I get my specialty or not," he asked annoyed, bringing me back to reality.

"Aight, specialty at ya house afta school."

"Dats whats up. A true hustla for real. Aight Lil' Shorty I'm out."

I continued to walk home when I heard some kids in back of me. They were some clown boys who wanted to be down, but had wack gear and could get no play. They're never gonna be down with me. But, I thought I heard someone say faggy ass and some kissing noises. I turned around and they were laughing running the other way. I turned around and kept walking thinking 'bout those new Lebron James tennis I would buy.

The next day after school I was going to the man with the purple bag house to get my hustle on when I ran into the dude he was in jail with on the basketball court.

"Hey Lil' Shorty," he said walking towards me.

"Hey what up?" I said.

"Where you going?" he asked bouncing a basketball.

"Going to handle sum business."

He laughed. "Oh so you back, huh?" he asked smiling.

"Something like dat."

"You got time fa me?" he asked looking around.

"I guess, I mean always got time for a customer," I said thinking about what the man with the purple bag had said 'bout going to da next niggah.

"Where at?"

"Yo, you sound like a *bidness man*," he said looking at me. "Aight, cool den. We can go in dat row house ova there, dats where the crack heads go to get high. Ain't nobody in there and it will be real quick, 60 bones right?"

"Yep, 60."

"Meet me in there in 'bout 5 minutes," he said and threw me the ball and walked away.

I bounced the ball and threw a few shots while I waited. A row house? A row house where crack heads go? Shit, I ain't wanna to go in there, but that $60 could go towards a jersey to go with my new tennis. My shit was better than that, but it is a quick $60. So I took my last shot and walked over there before I changed my mind.

It was a quick 60 bucks. Shit, I forgot about how much I missed the money. Man, let me hurry up to the man with the purple bag house before I miss out on the rest of my money. When I knocked on the door a lady answered. Guess it was his mom, but then I noticed something. All I did was just stare at her for a second. Her eyes were like my ma's.

"Honey, may I help you?" she asked smiling.

"No, I'm sorry," I said and ran home.

CHAPTER THIRTY-NINE

The Red-hair, Freckled-face Girl

Dear Diary,

My day was good at school. The boy I like is back. Guess what? He liked my card and even said thank you. But what really had me geeking was when he said sorry for pick'n on me when my period came through my pants. All I could say was thanx. Dat was nice of 'em, even Ms. Brown smiled. Then I came to the home and got some even more happier news. Ms. Betty got a letta from child services and we are going back to family court. My ma broke up with Big Boy and I may be able to go home because of my good behavior and sessions with Ms. Betty and the counselor. I tole my boo about the possibility of me going home an she was happy and sad. She asked me what about her and said I was gonna leave her. I tole her I would come and vis , write, call, and even meet her at the mall when they went every other Saturday. She wanted to know if I wanted to go home. I tole her yeah. Then she asked me some shit like why I wanna go home and then she kissed me. I miss my ma and my room, but I will miss you, to. I said when she kissed my neck. OMFG, she kept kissing me and umm she tasted like strawberries. Then guess what?...she stopped and went and closed the door. That is against the rules and I just knew someone was gonna come open it. They didn't and she didn't care. And then she turned off da lights. It was so dark and I couldn't see shit. She found me and kissed me again. I was trippin' 'cause I liked kissing her and she's a girl to. Dats the crazy part. She rubbed on my chest but not like Big Boy did. It was soft. She played with my egg drops. Dats what she calls 'em and sucked on 'em to. She put my hands on hers and I did what she did. I called her my teacher 'cause every thang I learned she taught me. She pushed me down on da bed and I got nervous. She tole me to take my pants and panties off. I was wearin' the ones she stole for me out VS. I wished the dayum lights was on so she could see 'em but whuteva. I was scared and I tole her dat. She tole me to remember what she said, that she would nevah let no one hurt me and dat was including her. She wanted to know if I trusted her and I tole her yeah. Den she said let me show you something and tole me dat she was doing 'dis 'cause she loved me. She loves me, yep. She said she loves me. I am her Redz, her baby. So I took down my pants and panties and threw 'em somewhere, dayum I wish she could have seen that I was wearing them. She got up off da bed, but then I felt her hand on my thighs, then I felt her hair on my thighs. She felt me in the dark and found my cat, dats what she called it. She got a name fa all my body parts. My lips she call candy and my butt she calls a pancake 'cause I ain't got no ass. But then I felt her tongue on it. She didn't do it like Big Boy, she was different. She was doing it 'cause she loved me and I loved her. Then shit got wild. I didn't know what was happening, but I started to pump up and down, I even grabbed her head and pushed her face into me. I couldn't help it, but then she stopped and said dats right Redz come for me and started again. I screamed and she told me to shhh so I covered my mouth and my body shook. She stopped and came up and kissed me. She didn't taste like strawberries. She tasted different. She tole me dats how she shows her love and she tole me I tasted good. She came and held me and said dats my Redz...always gonna be my Redz. I loved her. Maybe I shouldn't leave.

CHAPTER FORTY

THE BOY

Today in Health class Mr. King was talking about diseases. Everybody's parent had to sign a paper saying that we had their permission to talk about this in school. My Unk signed and told me I needed to know about shit like that and that school was the best place to hear about it rather than hearing it on the streets… like he did all fucked up and stuff.

The class was tripping. Mr. King collected all the papers and something like two kids' parents didn't sign, so he sent them to Mr. Mack's class. Mr. King then gave us some info on the different types of STDs and what they could do to our bodies. He even showed us some pictures and then we really started acting crazy. Things with bumps, and shit coming out them, and the girls' shit was nastier with bumps and puss and sores. Ah, it was so nasty. But what really got us tripping was the lady from the Health dept. She came in and talked about how many people our age had diseases and how to use condoms and latex if we gonna do oral sex. But then, she said stuff about licking ass or anus and dicks and the class was cracking up. Mr. King shook his head like he couldn't believe she just said that. I know I couldn't either. That's when somebody said he knows somebody in here who needs to know about this information. Everybody in class was cracking up. At first, I didn't pay it no mind 'cause everybody know that boy with the long nails and corn rows is a faggy. He hangs with girls and he acts like one, too. Mr. King told everybody to chill out before he gave us all detention. He told us to take something serious for once in our life. Then the lady from the Health dept. said that no matter if it was hetero- or homo-sexual sex we needed to be careful. And the same boy said that I would know 'bout homo sex. I knew this time he was talking about me. When I looked to the back of the room I saw him. It was that corny fat boy who was behind me when I was walking with the man with the purple bag the other day. He started laughing and saying I was a gay, a faggy.

"You better close ya mouth," I said looking dead at him, "before I fuck you up." All the kids was making noise and making oooh sounds.

"Da only thang you fuck'n is a man, you faggy. "We know what you be doin' wit him," he said laughing looking around at the other students.

I don't remember getting up, but I do remember the other kids yelling and laughing. I started punching him in his face and head. I know I was fuck'n him up because he was crying and bleeding. Mr. King tried to pull me off him, but I had him in a head lock. The other kids were screaming and jumping around. Then Officer Morrison came in and grabbed me and Mr. King grabbed the corny fat boy.

"Dayum, he beat da bricks off ya," said my Boy with the Mohawk.

"You got fucked up," said another girl.

"Who da faggy nah, bitch!" I said breathing hard trying to hit him again.

Mr. Thompson came in trying to control the class when Officer Morrison took me to the office and Mr. King took the corny boy to the nurse. I saw Mrs. Harris go in to help Mr. Thompson calm the class down. When we got to the office, Ms. Wilson was already in there.

"What happened?" she said walking up to me.

I didn't say anything. Officer Morrison told her about the fight. She asked Officer Morrison could she see me alone for a second and he nodded yes then she walked me to the back room.

"What in the hell happened? You just got back," Ms. Wilson said loudly.

I didn't say anything.

She grabbed me by my face and said, "You better say something or it's gonna be another fight between you and me," she said poking me in my chest.

I looked at her and said, "He called me a faggy."

"So that's what you're fighting about, him calling you gay? Did he touch you? Did he?"

"No. But he was saying that I be doing dudes. I ain't no faggy," I said getting mad all over again.

"Oh, I can't believe this," she said clapping one time. All of this over a word. If it's not true then who cares?"

But, in a way it was true. I was giving the man with the purple bag head and hand jobs. Was I a faggy?

Officer Morrison came in with Mrs. Harrison and Ms. Barnett, the principal, and asked Ms. Wilson to please excuse us.

"We will talk later," said Ms. Wilson, as she closed the door.

I was suspended for 10 days, and I had to wait to see if the corny boy's mom was gonna press charges. Dayum, I fucked up for some clown niggah. Unk came and got me. He was mad as hell. He screamed at me the whole way home. He was asking me what happened. Did someone say something 'bout Mom or my brother? I didn't say anything. He asked if somebody had called me out my name. I shook my head no.

"Den what they hatin' on you for? What da fuck you fight'n for?"

"Nah it ain't like that," I said looking away from him.

"Den what da fuck is it that got you kicked outta school for 10 days?"

I looked at Unk, but couldn't tell 'em the truth. I couldn't tell him that I was a faggy 'cause of what I was doing. My eyes filled with tears and I ran into the house and into my room where I stayed for the rest of the night.

CHAPTER FORTY-ONE

The Red-hair, Freckled-face Girl

Dear Diary,

When I got in from school today Ms. Betty tole me dat the court date was in 3 weeks. She said something about revaluating my file. She said that means they is gonna look in it to see if I am better or not. She took me in her office because she said she had some questions to ask me. She asked me how school was going and if the bathroom arrangement was working out. This the second time she said something about it and I had no idea what she meant. Then she started asking me about my friendship with the new girl. I tole her it was cool and that we have a lot of fun together. Then Ms. Betty asked me something weird. She wanted to know if I was having any sexual feelings. She said a "u" word, but I don't know what it was. She asked me did I want to touch anyone or had anyone been touching me. I lied and tole her no. I couldn't tell her dat me and my boo was kissing and stuff when we were in the room alone. I couldn't tell her that I sumtimes touch myself 'til I get dat shakin feelin I get wit my boo. If I tole her dat, my chances of going home would be fucked up so hell nah I ain't tell her.

Then she started asking me about my lil' brother and the situation dat had happened between us. I didn't want to talk 'bout dat. I hate thinking 'bout it.

I mean it wasn't like I hurt him. I was just curious. I would always give him a bath because Momma was too busy wit Big Boy or on da phone. I mean dayum, I just wanted to see if he would get hard like Big Boy did. When it did I guess I played with it 'til, I don't know. Shit, I was curious. My lil' brovah was laughin' da whole time. Still don't know how my momma found out or who called the protective service people. All I remember is Ms. Betty coming and tak'n me here. They said what I did was some type of assult to a child. But nobody did anything to Big Boy when I was scream'n he did it to me first. He said I was lying and held my movah who was crying. He was scream'n to get me out da house. What the fuck, he should be out not me. Anyway, I had tole Ms. Betty that I knew what I had done was wrong and I wouldn't do it again. She was smiling and shit. For real I would say anything to Ms. Betty to get da fuck outta here. She was glad and tole me if I keep up wit good behavior she don't see why I can't go home.

When I left her office I saw my boo and tole her the

good news. She just looked at me. She was like so I am really trying to leave and I tole her I wasn't leaving her, just going home. She was like how da fuck we gonna be together if I ain't gonna be here. I didn't say nutt'n 'cause I didn't have an answer. She left me standing there and she hasn't spoken to me since. I miss her. She hasn't even ate dinner wit me. She been hang'n with dat big butt girl who just came 'bout a month ago. What am I gonna do?

Chapter Forty-Two

Ms. Wilson and the Teachers

I left the office pissed off and walked straight to Brownie's room. It was our planning period and we normally ate lunch around this time with the Spanish teacher, Ms. Kragen and Ms. Counts, the other Language Arts teacher. I walked right in and they looked up to say "hey", then I went off.

"Can you believe that he was fighting because someone called him a faggy? Hell if that's the case I should have fought at least 10 kids this week for calling me a bitch."

"Who are you talking about?" asked Ms. Counts laughing.

"He is going to miss more work and it is just going to pile up and then what? God only knows what can happen in 10 days. Maybe the stress from his mom's passing gave him a short fuse and the name calling thing made him snap," she ranted, barely stopping to breathe.

"She is talking about her favorite student," Brownie whispered to the other two ladies. They both nodded their heads as they continued to listen. Ms. Counts, or "County" as she was tenderly called by this circle of colleagues and girlfriends because of her warm smile and auburn-colored curly hair, mouthed a silent "Oh".

"I mean, he has been under quite a bit of stress lately. It is hard coping without your mom, you know? But what about what the kids were saying? A couple of the girls did say that he was hanging around a man who just got out of jail and doing little "favors" for him. Is that really true? Could he be prostituting himself to men?" Willie said pacing and talking to no one in particular.

"Huh? Who? What? Oh what a thought, that's sick," said Ms. Kragen.

"A man using a young boy to do stuff like that, it is possible? We see it on Dateline every week, you know… "To Catch a Predator Series," said Ms. Counts agreeing with the other two teachers.

"Can you really believe what a child says, but why would they make up a lie like that?" Willie asked finally having a seat with the other three women.

"Okay, Willie now that you have calmed down some can you tell us what is going on and where is your lunch?" asked Ms. Kragen getting up.

"In my room. I forgot to pick it up when I left the office. I was so mad I walked right by my room," Willie said shaking her head.

"I'll get it, anything need to be warmed?" asked Ms. Kragen.

"Nope, I just have a salad today. Thanks K, appreciate it."

"Be right back. Don't start the story without me," Ms. Kragen said running out the door.

"Guess you didn't have a good day, huh?" Brownie said moving one of Willie's dreads out of her face and rubbing her back.

"It was going good until about 10 minutes ago," Willie said taking a deep breath.

"Okay, now you can start the story," said Ms. Kragen, handing Willie her lunch bag and sitting back down. Ms. Kragen, also known as "Senorita K" (because she taught Spanish) or "Ms. K" (to the students who couldn't pronounce her name correctly), was the youngest and the most enthusiastic about teaching of the bunch. This petite cookie-colored 23-year-old housed the tenacity every teacher possessed earlier on in their teaching career, resumed her spot back down at the table.

"That was fast, dag did you run? You are so damn energetic," said Brownie, "I don't know where you get it from. You're always jumping around or doing something. Makes me tired just looking at you.

"Girl, I'm always like this. I don't know, maybe it's being a newlywed that keeps me active, and makes me hyper, if you know what I mean?" Ms. K said in a Spanish accent.

"Nope, don't know what ya mean," said Brownie. "Ain't had none in 6 months."

"Ohhhh, umm girl, I don't know how you do it," said Ms. County covering her face with her hands.

"Me either. I couldn't get away with not letting Calvin get some for 3 days let alone 3 to 6 months," Willie said.

Just the thought of Calvin made her smile. The tension eased in her face and she began to breathe normally. Damn, that is how a man should affect you. He is supposed to make everything okay, and by the look on her face, Calvin did just that.

"Alright now, tell us what happened, Willie. I got a coverage after lunch," said County.

"God I hope I don't have one. Who's out now? I don't know why they won't just pay for a substitute," fussed Brownie.

"The new Music teacher has the flu or something. I have had her class before. She has seventh grade and they are off the hook. So I need some girl talk to get my mind right before I deal with rowdy children that I don't know," said Ms. County rolling her eyes.

"So what happened, Willie?" asked Ms. K.

"My favorite got into a fight today because somebody called him a faggy. Do you believe that he got 10 days for beating a boy up?"

"It had to be more than that Willie for him to get 10 days," said Ms. K biting her sandwich.

"Well Officer Morrison did say the other boy was hurt pretty bad, and he was bleeding. Morrison said by looking at the gash on his head the boy will need stitches."

"Dag, he got him pretty good. A gash in his head—geeez. Why would he beat up a boy that bad for calling him gay? There must be something to it," said Ms. K punching the air with her fists.

"Well, while he was out some of the kids were saying or reporting that he was hanging with some man who just got out of jail," said Brownie.

"I heard that, too, but then I found out that his uncle was just released a few months before his mother passed. So I figured that the man they were talking about was the uncle," said Willie.

"I heard something different, Willie," said County trying her best not to make eye contact.

"So what did you hear, County?" asked Brownie, nudging County in the arm.

"Well, umm, how do I put this? It's along the same lines as what you said Willie and…"

"County, please tell me, this is driving me crazy," pleaded Willie.

"Alright, well a few of the kids in my class were talking about this boy who was messing around with some men in the neighborhood. As soon as I heard that detail I shut down the entire conversation. So they keep it down. They kept it down alright because they started passing notes. When I saw one girl passing another girl a note, I made her give it to me. She didn't care because it wasn't about her, but the note was in great detail. Well, from the note, the girl's uncle has been messing around with a boy that goes to our school and the boys does, umm, gives hand jobs for $60. The note stated that her uncle's friend hooked him up with the boy about a month or so ago because he was getting serviced, too. The note also said that he had a scheduled appointment for his service."

"What the hell, get out of here! Are you sure they were talking about him?" asked Willie standing up.

"Yeah. She named him when the other girl begged her to tell her who it was. She also said that he has two other customers. One he also gives hand jobs to and the other he gives something called the 'specialty'."

"How does she know all of this? You know how some kids lie. If he is jerking these men off, where is he doing it and if he is doing it in their house somebody should have called the police on these perverts. How does she know this for sure?" Ms. K asked.

"Funny, the girl asked the same question and she told her that she overheard her uncle on the telephone while he was in the basement watching movies talking to one of his friends."

"I can't believe it; the boy is selling himself to men for money. He is a male prostitute in the eighth grade? This is way too much for me," said Ms. K totally blown away.

"I know. I gave the note to Mrs. Woodrow before I came here. She said she was going to pull the young lady first to see if she was telling the truth and then pull him."

"What is the world coming to? Our kids are growing up too fast. They don't have the opportunity to just be children," said Brownie. Children today are nothing like us. Remember when the biggest type of sexual flirtation, if you will, was when a boy hit your butt and ran off?"

"I know. A boy felt your booty and took off running if he liked you. Now boys take things to the extreme. At one time giving a boy a kiss was pressure, especially if he wanted you to french kiss him back then. Now boys don't want kissing. They want oral sex or just plain ole sex. If I had to be a teenager in today's world, with the types of peer pressures they face today, I don't think I would survive. Not to mention I was scared of sex and second I didn't have any kind of figure. Look at the young ladies we teach. Either they are overweight," said County.

"No tell the truth County," cutting her off, "they are fat because they eat all the wrong foods and don't exercise," said Ms. K.

"You're right, either they are fat or built like brick houses. Think about it how many fat kids were in your class in elementary or middle school? I can remember two," said County.

"I had two as well. It was like Noah's ark one fat boy and one fat girl. Then, you had one girl with big breast, but now they all have them," said Brownie.

"It's the hormones in Similac," said Ms. K. I read a research report in college that stated that Similac is full of hormones. Look at how they transform our girls into women by the time they are 13 and some cases as young as 10 or 11."

"What happened to good ole fashion breast milk? Healthy milk for growing babies," Brownie said trying not to laugh. Shoot, I was raised on breast milk and when I compare my physique to my nieces, who were strictly Similac babies, the differences are crazy. My oldest niece wears a 44 DD bra, size 10 shoe, and a 18 in pants and she is 16. Maybe I should play that for the pick-four lottery. I am 33 and wear a size 36 C bra, which I just recently started to wear. She got those things at 12. Now don't get me wrong, her momma was a drive-thru window bandit when it came to feeding her and that definitely helped, but I think the culprit was and is the Similac. It jump started her growth. In my fifth-grade class there was a girl name Randy Brooks and she had the biggest breasts I had ever seen on an 11-year-old. The boys loved to watch her when we played double dutch because they were watching her boobs bounce. Now the boys have a selection. They have several pairs of breast to look at and the bad thing is these girls are showing them."

"You're so right, for every class you had a certain kind of formula of kids. The fat one, the really skinny one, the girl with the big boobs, the dirty kid, and some boy with the curly hair," said County.

"Umm hum, the one who lived with his grandma because his parents were drunks. Remember when alcoholism was the substance abuse of choice in the eighties before crack?" Brownie recalled.

"Now a good number of our kids live with their grandma, auntie, uncle, or in groups homes because their parents are absent from their lives," replied Ms. K.

"What happened to the black family? Never mind, you already answered me—Crack. When the momma's are no longer in the houses then the children are left to make it on their own. Grandma is too old to really take care of them, but she tries. It's a shame because she has already raised her kids and now she must raise her grandkids in the age of technology," said County.

"Times have definitely changed," Willie said, after a long silence of listening and thinking. "Our family structure is damn near destroyed. Sex is glamorized and living the fast life is what our kids see every day on the news, in videos and magazines, and on-line," she said and sat back down. "Their innocence is lost so early. Now getting hit on the butt is not even a big deal anymore. The girls now do it to the boys. The roles are reversed. That practice went out of style when we were in high school. We have girls and boys giving head to show they like each other. Kids are bringing guns to school for protection or revenge. Kids are having sex before they turn 13 to show they love each other and children having sex for money. What do they have to look forward to when they become our age—nothing."

"Who do you blame, the media, the music artist, or the parents?" asked Ms. K. "Really, who can you blame?"

"To me, I blame all three, but the parents more so. The question that needs to be asked is how is sex being introduced to a child? Did the mom or dad tell them about sex and how it should be and not just the birds and bee's bull our parents told us? I mean, do parents tell their children that sex can be beautiful and not what you see in a porno with their friends? That sex can be dangerous? Do they talk about the diseases you can get from sex, along with pregnancy? Do they tell their children about good and bad touches? I am not saying that all children will be virgins, but they need to be aware of all aspects of sex, not just the ones parents are comfortable with. To this day, my mom has yet to have the sex talk with me. She told me about getting my period, but she didn't talk to me about sex and I am 33," ranted Brownie.

The three ladies sat for a second and looked at Brownie. She had never showed that much emotion about a topic that related to children. The silence seemed like a lifetime, while Brownie looked at her lunch for refugee. Ms. K broke the silence.

"But you have to remember, that back in the day black people didn't talk about sex, being gay, or if a relative was touching a child inappropriately. People always seemed to find out by happenstance or at the funeral when the person died. Think about it, your great aunt or grandma would say he use to touch lil' boys or she was always funny while snapping peas. It was like an afterthought. No one thought about how it may have affected the child later in life. That child kept things like that to themselves and there was no outlet to talk to anyone. Matter of fact, the black family didn't talk and in some homes they still don't talk. Things like that are kept quiet. It is still taboo," said Ms. K.

"You are right. Those same girls who were touched by *Uncle Bobby* are now promiscuous. They have experienced something unnatural. At first it's uncomfortable, then it becomes a regular routine, and before you know it they began to look for it elsewhere. It's almost like a person who gets that heroin high for the first time; they are forever chasing that first high and will never get it again. These children get the first taste of sex and their appetites are peaked and then they go from boy to boy trying to find that first weird, yet enticing, feeling," continued County.

The men aren't any better. It was funny when a boy would tell the story of how he lost his virginity. Their 16-year-old babysitter or a female cousin took their virginity. They have felt something so real that they stick their inexperienced underdeveloped penises into anything that is warm and pump, pump, pump until they climax and then it's off to the next one. But then what does that say about the girl who had sex with him? She is already messed up if she thinks that having sex with a 9-year-old boy is okay. She has already been touched by someone for her to continue the cycle of abuse. The sad thing is that the girl or the boy doesn't realize that what just happened is sexual abuse. Drying humping, finger popping, groping when you don't want to, and telling a child not to tell anyone is abuse. Its manipulation and abuse," said Willie with tears in her eyes.

"You're right. It is the same for boys as it is for girls. The way a boy is introduced to sex maps his future sexual encounters," Brownie said rubbing Willie's back controlling her own emotions. "You know last week I was in the barber shop getting my eyes brow done and the guys were watching CB-4... You know, the old Chris Rock movie where he was trying to be a gansta' rapper like Eazy E but straight outta low cash?"

"Oh yeah, and the guy who played G-money—oh what is his name—what is it?" said County.

"Yep, well the barber shop was full and this guy was in there with his two sons waiting for the next chair. Anyway, the sex scene came on and Chris was licking the woman's breasts and they started to have sex on the balcony. I told my barber, there are babies in here, why are you all watching this in the middle of the afternoon? All he could say was yeah I know, Kev put it on. Meanwhile, Chris is banging the hell out of this woman's back and I looked up and this boy who couldn't have been more than 7 was staring with his mouth open. The other boy who had to be 4 or 5 was looking, too. I asked was anyone going to cut this off. The response from the father was laughter and the typical male response of 'he'll be aight'. See, that's the stuff I am talking about. These two babies are being exposed to sex in the barbershop and who knows what is going on through their little minds. For all we know this is how sex offenders are created, through their introduction to sex," said Brownie. "It's not love. It's not beautiful. It was, excuse my language, it was fucking."

"But this boy has gone beyond just kissing, finger popping, or having sex with girls his age. He is doing things with and for grown ass men. If this note turns out to be true he has been manipulated into believing that jerking off and giving blow jobs to men is acceptable. Now he has to defend himself and his little eighth-grade reputation because people are saying he is gay," said Willie.

"Well at least now he can get some help. If it is true then we can get those dirty men and he can get the help he needs. At least Willie, you can help this one. Know that in your heart, he is going to be alright because now it is out. He is going to be alright," Ms. K chimed in rubbing Willie's arm.

"But the damage may have already been done. He has lost his mom, his brother is God knows where, and his uncle may not even know to help him. I hope you're right. I hope that Mrs. Woodrow will have something in place before he comes back from his 10-day suspension," Willie said.

"If she doesn't I am sure you will," said Brownie trying to lighten the mood.

"She will and we are here to help and pray, too," County said smiling. "Aight, chica's gotta go do this coverage. See ya afterwards," County said grabbing her lunch bag and giving Willie a quick hug.

"See ya," said the three ladies, all together.

The silence in the classroom was thick and screaming in all of our ears. "You wanna pray?" asked Brownie grabbing Willie's hand.

"Can we please?" urged Willie bowing her head and reaching for Ms. K's hand.

CHAPTER FORTY-THREE

The Red-hair, Freckled-face Girl

Dear Diary,

I have 10 days 'til we go to family court and I am starting to wonder if I really want to go home. Ms. Betty said that when I go home I will still have to do counseling, but wit my ma and lil' brother. She said we was gonna have to talk 'bout what went down between me and my brother. I don't wanna talk 'bout dat shit. But Ms. Betty said it would probably be ordered by the court, so I may have to. She asked me again today during our session if I was having any feelings that I wanted to tell her 'bout. I had tole her no. She noticed dat I hadn't been hanging wit my boo and wanted to know why. I tole her some bull shit, like you are right we do have different interests. Dat seemed to make her happy. Dayum, but I miss her. She still hanging wit dat big ass bitch. I see she got a fuck'n red weave in her head and be flinging dat shit when she wit my boo. She be touchin' it and stuff like dat shit is real. She should be touchin' my hair. Least my shit is real. Try'n to make dat <u>bitch look</u> like me. I tried talk'n to her at dinner and she was like can't you see I'm busy and dat big ass biotch started laugh'n. I tole her my bad, just thought you wanted to know about da court date. She played me right in front of dat big ass biotch. She was like look Shorty, you ain't gone yet? Ain't dat what ya court date 'bout. Den start early and get da fuck outta my face. I wanted to cry. Dat big ass girl was laugh'n and den my boo started laugh'n to. I didn't even eat dat night. I went straight to my room. I was so angry dat I ripped da panties she gave me. Maybe if she knew dat I wanted to stay she wouldn't be wit her and she would be wit me. Just when I was 'bout to close my door, I saw dem walking to my boo's room and she looked at me den shut da door. I wonder if she doin' to her what she did to me. She can't because she said she loved me. I'ma show her I love her still. I can't wait to go to the mall this Saturday. I'ma hook my boo up.

CHAPTER FORTY-FOUR

THE BOY

It has been real quiet since I got suspended. I pretty much stayed in my room when Unk was home. He would wake me up before he went to work to tell me what chores I had to do around the house and told me to make sure I do the work the school sent over while I was home. Most of the time, I went right back to sleep when he left, but I did clean up when I got up. I just knew when I got suspended Unk was gonna beat my ass, but he didn't. I guess he thought since Moms hadn't been gone that long, that I was just acting out or just still trying to get over her not being here. Yeah, part of that was true, but I couldn't tell him what the real truth was. I did most of the work the school sent and spent the rest of the day playing on my Wii. One day, while I was walking to the store, I ran into the man with the purple bag.

"Ay, Lil' Shorty, what up?" he asked while drinking something.

"Nutt'n" and I kept walking. He was the last person I wanted to see. It was because of him that people at school was calling me a faggy.

"Oh, you ain't got time to speak to ya best customer?" he asked grabbing my arm.

"Yo, get the fuck off me!"

"Don't pull away from me you lil' shit. I'm da reason you got hot shit and a pocket full of money. Shit. Don't you know da customer giveth and da customer taketh away? I made you, motha fucka, and I can break you. You betta recognize," he said spitting his words and letting me go. "I hear you got suspended for fight'n some boy. Heard you fucked 'em up, too," he said taking another drink.

I just stood there breathing hard.

"Look niggah, don't swell ya chest up ova here 'cause I will pop dat shit," he said acting like he was popping a balloon. "I was just conversating with ya. Shit. Anyway, since you outta school and shit, den I can get hooked up daily. So I'ma be by today to get da specialty, cool?" he asked sucking his teeth.

"Nah," I said and walked away.

"Oh, it's like dat?" he asked screaming. "Oh, so you wanna niggah to go get his shit from anotha niggah, huh? Aight Lil' Shorty, I got ya. Niggah, I got ya."

Instead of going to the store, I decided to go home. I didn't know what I was going to do. I know the shit I do for the man with the purple bag and his boy is fucked up, but I like the money. I mean, I get to buy what I want and I stay fresh, but now people are starting to talk and I don't like how it's turning out. What if my brother hears about it? What will I do then? But the money is good. Maybe if I just do it a couple more times this week, then I won't do it again. I will be straight. Besides, the school year is almost over and I will be going to high school and I know Unk will get me some fresh gear for that. He always says how high school is a different ball game. Maybe if I just do it a couple more times.

CHAPTER FORTY-FIVE

The Red-hair, Freckled-face Girl

Dear Diary,

I am fuck'n up. Today we went to da mall and I had a plan. When we got to da mall Ms. Betty needed to know who our partners was gonna be. My boo was wit dat big ass bitch and I went with the girl who digs in her nose. She da one who got put in here fa burning down her grandpa's house. She was the only one left by the time everybody else had picked. So I tole her she could follow me to the store I wanted to go in and then I would follow her. Dat dumb bitch just stared at me with her finger in her nose. I swear I think she ate a boogey, nasty bitch. So we went to Victoria Secret first and she was looking at the lotions digging in her nose and wiping it on shit. The sales lady was looking at her making faces, but she ain't say nutt'n to her. So I went and found the panties my boo had and picked up some nightgowns and bras. I had a small piece of foil in my pocket. I put da shit on like she showed me and then just walked out. I told the boogey girl lets go, she flicked a boogey at the sales lady and left. She thought that shit was funny. I didn't wit her nasty ass. So I had her a bra and panty set. That's all I was gonna get her until I saw some cute shorts dat I knew she would like in Aeropostle. I had another small piece of foil left dat I was gonna use to get me some earrings, but dis was to get my boo back so I went in there. The boogey girl followed me but she sat on the bench outside da store. Dat was good cause watching her pick her nose was making me sick. I grabbed a whole bunch of shit and went into the dressing room. I had on sweat pants so da shorts fit and just when I was walking telling da boogy girl lets go the alarm went off. This guy dressed in some jeans and a hoody walked up to me and asked me to empty my pockets. I was gonna argue with him, but that was only gonna make it worse. Shit I got caught today. The boogey girl stopped digging in her nose and went and found Ms. Betty. They took me in the back and the guy in the hoody who was a cop said he noticed the tag hang'n out of the back of my sweatpants. The alarm just made it worse. Ms. Betty came in and she was mad as shit. She talked to the police officer and he wrote up some report. They made me take off da shorts and when I came back in the room. I had to take a picture. They tole me I was not allowed back in da store or they would arrest me. Shit. I fucked up, but at least they didn't find the panties and bra I got from Victoria Secret. I still had a nice present for my boo. Ms.

Betty screamed on me all the way back to the home. The boogey girl just looked at me, she was mad because we didn't get to go to Hot Topic like she wanted. When we got back to da home, Ms. Betty called me into her office to tell me she had to put this in my file and this was not going to look good in court. Shit, I had forgot about dat. She also said that for as long as I was here, my free time would be limited and I would get more chores. Shit dat meant I wouldn't be able to spend time with my boo. When I left Ms. Betty's office, I went to my room and took off da stuff I had for boo. I got dressed and went to her room. Her door was closed. I knocked and then opened it. The girl wit dat big ass was in dere. Boo looked at me like she didn't want to see me. I tole her I got her a gift and handed it to her. She looked at it and gave it to dat big ass girl. She said thanx she will look real nice in it tonight and licked her lips. I wanted to die. She gave her the shit I got for her and gave it away right in front of me. I screamed at her about her saying she wouldn't hurt me. She said she need in house love not out house love and told me to get out. Da big ass girl laughed at me and waved bye bye. I was crying right in front of her and she turned the music up and laid back with her eyes closed. I couldn't believe she did that. I got caught stealing for her and she doesn't even care. I may not be able to go home 'cause of dat shit. What do I do now? I can't stay here? I gotta figure something out.

CHAPTER FORTY-SIX

THE BOY

I forgot how much money I made from my hustle and he didn't even take that long this time. Normally my arm is tired, but not today. The man with the purple bag told me he missed my skills and that it was worth another buck for my time. He was high, drunk, and quick. Only a little came out this time so it didn't take me long to clean up. If I do it a couple more times at 300 a pop, I won't ever have to do shit no mo. Fuck them $60 hand job dudes, I'm gonna up the price on them, too, if they want my services.

The walk home was quick. I got back in the house by 11:30. Dayum, I was only gone like 30 minutes. I saw the man with the purple bag yesterday and he wasn't mad at me. He said he understood why I felt funny. He said he did too up Jessup, but he told me that survival is the name of the game. You gotta have money to live out here in these streets and that's why everybody got or need to have a hustle. The people selling water on North Ave. in the summer, the Chinese people selling flowers, even the Muslim men selling the newspaper and bean pies. He told me that my hustle is just different and for a certain type of customer. When I thought about what he said it made sense. He even let me come to his house when I wanted to. I kept thinking about those new Lebron James' tennis and decided I would just go and he was home.

When I got in the house the message light on the telephone was blinking, it was probably Unk calling to see if I cleaned up the bathroom. When I checked the messages, putting in my mom's name as the code, it wasn't Unk who left the message, but Mrs. Woodrow from school. She wanted Unk to call her because there was something she wanted to talk to him about. Shit, I was in enough trouble without her telling him something else like I am failing and probably need to go to summer school or that I may have to stay back because of my grades. She would just have to keep calling back until he answered the telephone, because I was deleting that message. Now there are no messages and I need to clean the bathroom before Unk gets back. Besides, I wanna get those tennis shoes today, too. I hope they got my size. Them things is hot.

CHAPTER FORTY-SEVEN

Ms. Brown

Sticks and stones may break my bones, but words will never hurt me. That is a bunch of bull. That's what we use to say when we were kids and it was and still is a lie. Kids called each other dummy, dirty, stinky, or even small, and the response would be someone giving you the finger, laughing it off, cussing you out, or saying something just as mean. For a while, I believed that saying until I got older and realized that words do hurt. I realized that those types of retaliations were just a cover up. A cover up that got bigger and bigger as I got older. I wonder if that's why I became a teacher, to take up for the unpopular, corny kids who are picked on like I was. After being molested by my cousin, I wonder did his words lead me to the dark places of my past. Words are the things that can break your spirit, lower your self-esteem, and haunt you for life.

Words hurt. The reason why talk shows are still popular is because of what people say to one another. We still have a Roman mentality. We love to see people argue, verbally purge, fight, and belittle each other. Instead of watching someone get eaten by a lion or beheaded, we watch them kill each other emotionally and spiritually with words. That's why Maury Povich and Jerry Springer are still on the air. To me, verbal abuse is worse than getting hit. Your swollen eye or lip will go down, a broken arm will heal, but you never forget when someone has said something hurtful. I am a verbally abusive person when I take on the defensive or when I am not thinking about the words that come out of my mouth. Hurtful words break friendships and relationships. I have lost a few friends and created a few enemies because of it. I think about how my father would sometimes call my mom stupid or naïve, and the look on her face showed that she was hurt. I really believe that characteristic was passed down to me from him. Is that where my quick wit and sarcastic remarks come from, my past pain? His past pain? My dad? So how do I transfer that pain? I do it in teaching.

When a student picks on another student, I verbally come to his or her rescue, like I wish someone had done for me. Kids are cruel. Their words are sharper than any two-edge sword and they don't care who gets cut. Maybe that is why I made sure that the boys didn't tell anyone about the red-hair, freckled-face girl's period coming through her clothes. I know what I said wasn't 'professional', but sometimes you gotta go there with these kids because that's what they understand. Street recognizes street. Once they know that you're not playing, respect is elevated. They won't fuck with you or anyone you may protect. Besides, she would have never lived that down. I know I didn't. That little girl is one of four other white students in this predominately black school. Not even enough of them to create a subgroup for white on the Maryland State Assessment. She has bright red hair, wears glasses for reading, she wears her uniform every day, she doesn't have the body these other girls possess, and she is quiet. They would have eaten her alive, not to mention the baggage she is carrying.

She would have never been able to live that down. I didn't and I was a little stronger than she is. I had a girl standing in back of me and saw the blood spot on my peach and white petal pushers and she didn't say a word. They laughed at me for the rest of the day until my teacher told me that I had a red spot on the back of my pants. It is small, but visible. It was too late to do anything because we were about to be dismissed from school. I couldn't figure out why people were laughing, but by the end of the day I understood. To this day I am very period conscience and I make sure that even at 33 my pants stay spot free. Funny how we see pieces of our former selves in the children we teach; every teacher does. I see some of me in her.

I am worried about Willie and about how emotionally involved she is with this young man. I know she wants to save him, but he has so much shit with him that she may be the one who drowns. I know she is reliving the death of her own mother. She does with every special event and probably every day. But this one she has taken to heart. So I am going to have to watch her and make sure she is okay for her sake and the boy's. She really sees something in him and she wants to help him. I am just not sure if he is beyond help.

The boy he beat the hell out of ended up getting 22 stitches in his forehead. The mom may press charges because she thinks the boy is dangerous. No, actually, if her son had kept his mouth closed, he wouldn't have gotten his ass kicked. Words hurt. That boy didn't even realize the pain he was inflicting by calling him a faggy. Technically, what he is doing is an act of homosexuality and if you just looked at it from that point of view then, yep, he is gay walking in the shoes of a down low brotha at 14. I have read books by E. Lynn Harris and J L

King about this type of lifestyle and it makes me mad just thinking about it. Grown men leading double lives, but a child? I never pictured it manifesting at such an early age. Willie needs to watch how she handles this and watch what she says to him during this meeting Mrs. Woodrow is trying to schedule. Words, once they float out of your mouth and permeate the atmosphere can never be taken back. The boy with the 22 stitches learned that the hard way.

What words did this man say to a 14-year-old boy that convinced him to perform sexual acts on him and other men? Anything I guess, these kids are so impressionable now a day. Whatever the man said, his words have altered this boy's life for the rest of his life. Dayum words. The power words possess are immeasurable and the destruction it causes leaves some damaged for life.

"Hi ma'am, are you ready to order now?" asked the blond hair bubbly waitress.

"Oh, I'm sorry. I am still looking at all the wonderful choices. Can I have a few more minutes?"

"Sure. Take your time. I'll be back."

"Thanks." Huh, sticks and stones may break your bones, but words will get your ass kicked.

CHAPTER FORTY-EIGHT

MS. WILSON

Mrs. Woodrow has been calling his house for the last 3 days, leaving messages, and no one has returned her calls. This is getting frustrating. After she pulled in the girl about the note she found out that there is enough information to call Child Protective Services. Mrs. Woodrow believes that this is going to be rather difficult because he has not admitted to anyone that he is being abused. She is going to call one more time and if he doesn't respond she is going to have to call them.

I know she is taking a big risk; she should have called the same day, but I begged her to give me a day or two to see what I could find out and then call. She knew that I had a pretty good relationship with them, so she did.

I went by the house twice and no one answered the door. I was going to leave a note, but decided against it, as if he would get it anyway. I called the number that we have on file in the main office and I get the dayum answering machine. I know somebody got those messages. I wonder does he know. Perhaps he had been erasing them. Would he do that?... Possibly so, if he doesn't want his uncle to know. Kids can be sneaky. Maybe he liked the money he was making? Maybe he is just gay? Nah, he likes flirting too much with the girls, but so do some men who are bisexual. AHHHH, this is too much. Too many unanswered questions.

"Hey Babe, you coming to bed soon?" Calvin called from the bedroom interrupting my thoughts.

"Yeah Babe, grading these tests and you'd think I didn't teach anything. Be in, in a minute."

F—it, I am going to the house before I go in tomorrow. I can't take this anymore. I need some answers before the meeting and I need them sooner than later. I am sure someone will be home when I knock on the door at 7 a.m.

CHAPTER FORTY-NINE

The Red-hair, Freckled-face Girl

Dear Diary,

The week is almost over and I am so glad. I go to court next week and I can't wait to go home. I am so sick of seeing my boo wit her. If she is trying to make me jealous, well dat shit is working. I can't even focus in school no mo. I ain't did my homework all week and the class work I been handing in I ain't finished. Ms. Brown has been writing bad shit on my progress sheet and Ms. Betty keep asking me what is wrong. She tole me dat those progress sheets go in my file fa court. I don't even care no mo. Last night when dat bitch got out da shower she put on da bra I got for my boo. She looked at me and rolled her eyes and said something like hata. I ran after her and grabbed dat red weave and we went at it. I was scratching at her face and all she was doing was yelling. Somebody was scream'n fight and den it seemed like everybody came in. Ms. Betty and Mr. James came in and broke us up. I had a hand full of dat weave in my hand and she was crying. My boo looked at me all crazy like, but I was so mad I would'a fucked her up to. Ms. Betty took me to the time out room. I hate dat room. Its dark and it freaks me out. I was fight'n Ms. Betty try'n not to go in there and I hit Ms. Betty in her face. She looked at me like I had really hurt her. I didn't mean to I just didn't want to go in there. Den Mr. James picked me up and slammed me on the bed in the time out room and closed da door. I couldn't breathe and I was banging on da door. They wouldn't let me out. I didn't know how long they was gonna keep me in dere. I was tripp'n. Then all of a sudden I thought about my boo and how she tasted like strawberry and how I would shake when she licked me and so I played wit myself. I rubbed and scratched so hard that it hurt. I was going crazy wit it and then I shook like I do wit her. When I finished I just laid there wit my hand on it. My hand felt wet. After about, I don't know how long, I was in dat time out hell hole, they took me to my room. I need to take a shower because my panties felt wet. No one else was in da bathroom but me, and when I went to take off my panties I realized that it wasn't cum, but blood. Dayum, had I rubbed dat hard? Am I tripp'n dat hard?

Chapter Fifty

The Boy

Dayum, I stayed too long today. Got home late 'cause we had to wait for the lady with the funny looking eyes to leave the house. She ain't ask no questions because she knew Unk and she knew that they are home boys. So, I just played on his Xbox and chilled. By the time I got home, Unk was there. He was sitting on the couch looking mad as shit. Dayum, I forgot to do those dishes.

"Hey, Unk, my bad. I'ma get on them dishes right now," I said walking straight to the kitchen.

"Where you been?" Unk asked.

"Oh, umm went to my boy's house to play Madden," I said, cleaning off some plates.

"You been at ya boy house all day. He ain't go to school today?" Unk asked walking into the kitchen leaning on the wall.

Unk was holding something in his hand and hitting his leg with it, and from what I could see it has the school's letters on it.

"Nah, I went to his house after school," hoping Unk would believe me.

"You lying," Unk said hitting the paper against his head.

"No I'm not, Unk. I didn't leave until about 2:30."

"Yo, why da fuck you lying? I been home since noon."

I dropped the plate in the sink and it broke. Unk walked closer to me and I froze.

"I'ma ask you dis question one more time. Where you been today?"

Before I began to speak, Unk handed me the paper he was holding and went and sat down at the table.

"Did you know we had a visitor today? Ya teacher, Ms. Wilson, came by here like 7 o'clock in da morning. You probably didn't hear, huh? 'Cause you was knocked out. She said the guidance counselor up at da school been calling all week leaving messages and shit and I ain't returned her telephone calls. So Ms. Wilson thought she would come by in person to find out why. Did the guidance counselor lady, Ms. Woodrow, call?"

I panicked and I was about to put da paper on da counter.

"Nah, hold on to dat," Unk said pointing to the paper shaking his head.

"Unk, she called and I thought I was in trouble. My grades are bad and..."

"So she did call and you erased the messages? All five messages, even the ones from Ms. Wilson?"

I nodded yes.

"Aight, open dat paper up and read it out loud to me."

I felt the tears, but wouldn't let 'em fall. I opened the paper and began to read to myself as Unk recited the words aloud.

"My uncle said he jerks him off for 60 bones," the paper fell out of my hands and onto the floor.

CHAPTER FIFTY-ONE

The Red-hair, Freckled-face Girl

Dear Diary,

Today is not da day to fuck wit me. I am walking funny 'cause my cat hurt and I didn't sleep good afta being in time out all dat time. Dat shit fucks wit me when I come out of dere. I hate being in dat room. Ms. Brown was standing in da hall saying good morning to everybody. I don't feel like dat shit or her today.

"Good morning," said Ms. Brown.

I just looked at her like she wasn't there.

"Excuse me, I said good morning. You're not speaking this morning?"

I shook my head no and went into the room.

"Um no progress sheet today?" she asked. This bitch is on my nerves already. I shook my head no and kept walking.

When she came in she started yapping right off da back. She was talking 'bout some pronoun shit and den I blocked her ass out. All I could think about was how fucked up shit was. After a while I put my head down.

"Are you okay?" asked Ms. Brown, coming over by my desk.

If I don't say something this bitch is gonna bother me all day. "I don't feel well and I gotta go to the bathroom."

"Umm, ah, okay let me call someone to take you to the nurse."

"I ain't gotta go to da nurse. I gotta go to the bathroom," I said annoyed.

Ms. Brown had walked over to her desk and picked up the phone and dialed somebody. I got up and went over to Ms. Brown when she held up her finger and told me to wait one minute. I stood there looking at her like 'dis bitch don't see I gotta pee.

"Look, I need to go to the bathroom, it's an emergency," I said getting louder.

Ms. Brown's eyebrow popped up when she hung up the phone.

"Don't get loud, alright? Mrs. Woodrow is on her way to take you to the nurse's suite so you can go to the restroom. Okay?" said Ms. Brown talking low. She was being to fuck'n calm for me. That ain't like her.

"Why da fuck do I need to go to da nurse. All y'all been talking about me going to da nurse when I gotta pee. You, Ms. Betty, Mrs. Woodrow, all y'all...What da fuck dat about?" I said waving my hands in her face. "Shit, is something going on and nobody told me? Ain't nobody else going to da nurse to pee."

"For real, I don't know who you think you're talking to, but you betta bring it down, 'cause I am not the one," Ms. Brown said and she wasn't, but I already was out there so fuck it.

"Whateva Ms. Brown, I gotta pee and I am going to the bathroom and not the nurse. Fuck that nurse and fuck you," I yelled and walked out the door.

AFTER READING

Determine what is important...

CHAPTER FIFTY-TWO

Ms. Brown

"Oh, what a day," said Brownie putting down her lunch on a student's desk. "You won't believe what just happened."

"Hey lady... Heard you had a confrontation in class today," said Ms. K.

"I heard the kids talking about your class on their way to lunch. What happened?" asked County.

"Where is Willie? I only want to tell this story once, because I want to keep my cursing to a minimum. I am trying to get my soul right with God."

"Oh shoot, it's that type of story, what..." giggled County.

"Hey guys gotta eat fast. I have a Parent-Teacher conference when this parent shows up," said Willie pulling out her chair.

"Okay, I guess today is full of gossip," said County biting into her sandwich.

"Oh yeah, 'cause I have got to tell you what I did," said Willie. "But what other gossip is there?"

"Well, I told you guys that the red-hair, freckled-face girl has gone back to her old ways? Not handing in homework and incomplete class work, right?" Brown said looking at the women, waiting for confirmation.

"Yep," said Ms. K.

"Well, today the shit hit the fan. She came to class with the biggest attitude to date. I haven't really bothered her, but you guys know how I feel about being ignored by a child."

"Oh Lord," said Willie. "She's ignoring all of us. I saw her in the hallway and asked her a question and she literally just looked at me like I was invisible."

"Umm humm. Well, I said 'good morning' and asked for her progress sheet. She ignored me. I was alright with that because we know how middle school kids are in the morning. No, let me rephrase that, she gave me a head nod for responding to two questions. No, she was not saying good morning and no she didn't have her progress sheet. Okay whatever, but then she laid on the table. That totally annoys me, but I play it cool. I went over and asked her what was wrong and she said she didn't feel well and she needed to go to the bathroom. Now guys, when we say a kid's got baggage, she *gots* baggage. So I follow the arrangements that are in place. Oh, I guess she was tired of walking all the way to the nurse's suite to go to the bathroom."

"Wait a minute Brownie, she can't go to the bathroom on her own?"

asked County.

"Nope. And all I will say is, sexual abuse where the prey becomes predator okay?" replied Brownie with her eyes wide open. It was quiet for a while when it seemed like everybody's eyebrows jumped to the sky.

"You mean, she is now the one being watched?" asked Ms. K.

"Oh dayummmmm, that's messed up. So that is why she is in the home?" asked County nodding her head.

"See, this is exactly what I am talking about! Who is taking care of our children? What the hell is going on in our society?" asked Willie cutting up her salad.

"Will explain later… Anyway, she gets mad when I tell her to wait because the counselor is on the way. She totally flips out. She got loud and was yelling about 'what the fuck is going on 'cause *ain't nobody told her*. The kids in the class are in shock, because they know I'm crazy and this little girl is yelling and cussing at me."

"That's the truth," said Willie laughing. "She was cursing and you let her live?"

"I can't deny it either. But, the little girl said fuck me and the nurse."

"No she didn't. She said 'fuck you' loud enough for you and the class to hear?" asked County.

"Both. Then she left the room. Girl, you know I was hot. I let her ass go, because for one she ran and for two, I probably would beat her like her momma should have if I caught her."

"Dag, where is she now?" inquired Ms. K.

"They are looking for her now. When I walked the kids to lunch, I saw Officer Morrison and Mr. Terry looking around the building for her. I went to Mrs. Woodrow's office and she was on the telephone with her counselor, Ms. Betty. She told me that she was on her way here. Ms. Betty told her that last night she was put in some time-out room and had hit her in the process."

"Oh, she is off the hook all the way around. In school and at the home-dag," said County.

"But get this, she goes to family court next week, with the possibility of going home and now with all the craziness she may have to stay."

Just then the intercom sounded... *Ms. Wilson can you report to the conference room? Ms. Wilson can you please report to the conference room?*

"Dag and I hadn't told you guys what I did this morning. I will see you guys in a few. This is going to be crazy."

"What is gonna be crazy? Give us the short version Willie," said Ms. K pleading.

"Okay, but real quick," said Willie while putting her container back in her lunch bag and grabbing her keys. "I went to his house this morning before work."

"Before work! You went to that boy's house at around... uh, 7 a.m.?" shouted Brownie. "Girl, are you crazy or just that determined?"

"I had to know why no one was returning my calls or Mrs. Woodrow's call. She was calling CPS today. I had to do something. Come to find out, he erased the messages that Mrs. Woodrow and I left. The uncle didn't know, and I left a copy of the note from his Health class with him. The meeting is with Mrs. Woodrow, Mrs. Harris, the uncle, him, and I."

"Oh my god! The uncle didn't know? He probably wants to kill somebody."

"Okay guys, I gotta go. Don't want them waiting. Will see ya at the end of the day. Let's go have a drink later. I have a feeling I may need one."

"Shoot, you got it. I know I'ma need me a glass of wine after listening to yall," said County.

"A glass, humph, the bottle," said Brownie. "Go to your meeting. We'll be here."

"Okay, see ya," Willie said and dashed out of the door.

"There goes our friend again with the superwoman cape flying in the wind. Her mission—Saving the children of the world," said Brownie.

"Only who is gonna save her?"

Chapter Fifty-Three

The Boy

Unk was quiet all the way home. He didn't really look at me, either. I can't believe he knows what I been doing with the man with the purple bag and his boys. Our walk home seemed longer because we took a different way home. I hadn't seen this side of the neighborhood, but I wasn't saying shit.

The whole time during the meeting with Mrs. Woodrow, Mrs. Harris, and Ms. Wilson he just sat there and listened. Mrs. Woodrow seemed to ask all of the questions and Unk was looking like he wanted to kill her. I ain't never seen him so mad, even when he fought my brother and broke the table. I didn't know what he was thinking. I didn't know what anybody was thinking. We all sat there in this circle. Unk and Ms. Wilson on opposite sides of me and Mrs. Woodrow and Ms. Harris across from me. I wanted to run out of there, but I knew somebody would have blocked me and caught me by the arm. Everybody just seemed to stare at each other and then at me. It made me nervous. I was so nervous my leg was bouncing every time somebody asked me a question. Unk would breathe harder with each question and his eyes seemed to bug out when I answered. I thought he was gonna hit me when he put his hand out, but he just put his hand on my leg to make me stop jumping. That was the only time he moved or made any physical contact with me.

When Mrs. Woodrow asked me when and where did it start, I didn't respond. I didn't want to say. Unk gave me this look out the corner of his eye like—niggah you better say something. She kept telling me this is no time to lie or withhold information because the problem won't get solved with lies or silence. She was like everyone is here to help me get out of a bad and unhealthy situation. Ms. Wilson was like yeah, it's okay now… Tell us so we can help end this mess. Everybody except for Unk was nodding their heads yeah, like one of my bobble heads. I was so mad. Mad at Ms. Wilson because if she hadn't come to the house we wouldn't be here right now. Mad at the girl for writing the note in Health class. Mad at myself for getting caught. This was worse than getting caught by the police. This was all fucked up! From what Mrs. Woodrow said, they were going to call Child Protective Services and the police if Unk still didn't respond to the calls they were making. Unk looked at me like he wanted to choke me. They looked at Unk and he didn't say anything, so Mrs. Woodrow asked her question again. How and where did I start?

I told them about the time Unk and his boys were down stair watching pornos and then the man with the purple bag came up stairs. Unk's eyes got real wide and he made a face like he remembered that day and then he balled up his fist, but he never said anything. I think Ms. Wilson saw it too 'cause she ask Unk was he okay and would he like a bottle of water. He shook his head yes and no.

Then Mrs. Woodrow began to ask questions that I really didn't want to answer like, what did I do and to who, how much was I paid, and where did I do it? When I said at the house, sometimes Unk started breathing hard. When I told them what I got paid for doing hand jobs and 'my specialty', I heard Ms. Wilson say something like oh my god and covered her mouth and Mrs. Woodrow just shook her head. Mrs. Woodrow wanted to know what the 'specialty' was and when I told her Ms. Wilson gasped like she couldn't breathe. Mrs. Harris dropped her pen on the floor. Unk just sat there holding the arms of his chair so tight his knuckles were lighter than the rest of his hand. His leg began to bounce real hard. I didn't touch his leg to stop his like he did mine 'cause I didn't know what he would do. Mrs. Woodrow was like, this explains why you were so angry when the other boy called you a faggy. I nodded my head and she wrote something down on her note pad. Mrs. Harris who really didn't say much, was constantly writing stuff down. The last two questions Mrs. Woodrow asked pushed Unk over the top. She asked me how many times I thought I had done this and how much money had I made? It took me a second to remember all the times and count. I started counting with my fingers while trying to remember the places I had done it up to just this week. I told her maybe five or six times with the man with the purple bag 'cause I made like $1200 with him and then with the other two dudes maybe three to four times each and I made about $400 with them. Unk jumped up, knocking his chair to the floor, and left the room. I guess he just couldn't take it anymore. He didn't say anything when Mrs. Woodrow called his name, but she didn't go after him either. Mrs. Wilson, Mrs. Harris, and Mrs. Woodrow looked at each other strangely and Mrs. Harris got up and went after him. I heard her calling his name when she closed the door. Ms. Wilson held my hand and told me everything would be alright, but I knew different.

When we got to the house, Unk went straight upstairs to his room and closed the door. I didn't want to go up because I couldn't face him. When he looked at me he looked like I made him sick. Like I was one of those faggy boys that walk up and down Charles Street at night dressed like women. If he wasn't going to leave me before when Momma died, he was probably going to leave me now. He doesn't want to be around no faggy. I heard his door open and close and he came down the steps. When he got to the bottom, he had on a hoody and was zipping it up. I sat down on the couch and looked at the floor. It was quiet for a while, just like it was when me and my brother had that argument about him giving Mommy chocolate city when she was sick. That quiet led to us not speaking and him not coming home. I didn't know where this silence was going to leave me and Unk. For it to be so quiet, it was loud as hell in my head. Unk walked over to me and when he raised his hand I jumped?

"What da fuck you jumpin' fa?" Unk asked me putting his hand back down.

"I don't know. Thought you was gonna hit me."

"Hit you? Nah, I ain't gonna hit you. Hit you fa wut?"

"'Cause of what Mrs. Woodrow told you today. 'Cause of what I been doing," I said quietly looking down at the floor.

"What I tell you 'bout lookin' at da floor? A real man look you straight in da eye. Now man up and look me in my eye."

He told me to man up. He still thought I was a man? After what he just found out about me? I looked up at Unk.

"I knew something was up. I peeped the new gear, the new tennis, and the money you would leave in ya pockets. I saw the money sometimes before I washed ya pants. I just thought ya brovah was giving you money so I didn't question it. He is ya brovah and I thought he was lookin' out fa you since ya ma died. So I ain't say shit to you or him. I just took it as a brovah loving and takin' care of his lil' bro like he should. Like he promised ya ma."

"What ya mean like he promised Ma? He never went to see her at that place, did he?"

"Yeah he did. He just went in da morning when you was at school. I ran into him one day and he was sittin' by her bed brushing her hair, telling her she had to stay hot," Unk wiped away a tear before it fell. "He saw me and was 'bout to leave and I asked him could we talk. Could we squash whateva beef we had befo' she left us? Could we make it cool right there in her room in front of her? Tole him I wasn't tryna be nobody daddy, just tryna be his fam. We squashed it that day. He tole ya ma that he would always look out fa you and that you would always get what you needed. See, dats where I thought you was getting ya bank from. Shit, but I didn't know it was dat much, I didn't know…" Unk stopped talking and just looked at me. "I tole my baby sis I would take care of ya'll and man shit…" his eyes were getting red. He rubbed the top of my head like he was trying to get something off of it. He put his hood on and said he'd be back and went out the door.

CHAPTER FIFTY-FOUR

The Red-hair, Freckled-face Girl

Dear Diary,

Dat fuck'n bitch should have just let me go to the bathroom like I wanted. But no I gotta go to the nurse to pee. Wut kinda shit is dat? Ms. Betty and Mrs. Woodrow know about dis bathroom shit and ain't nobody say nuttin' to me. Shit is fucked up. I know she probably know now. She gotta know. Why else do they want me to pee in the nurses office? Dats why Ms. Betty keep asking me about stupid sexual feelings. Dem fuck'n bitches. They just like my movah, don't tell me shit just make me do dumb stuff and act like I should just keep it moving. Shit, dere go Officer Morrison. Shit, and he is wit Mr. Terry to. Fuck, dat bitch Mrs. Woodrow probably got dem lookin' for me like I'm some dayum criminal. I'ma go down to the A-wing and go to the sixth grade hallway. They look like dey going to the C-wing.

Dat's real stupid. You got men trying to find me, but they can't go into da girls bathroom. I can stay in here all day and they wouldn't find me in here. Ain't nobody in here either shit, I'm straight. Oh shit!

"Huh," said a little Spanish girl with a long black pony tail in braids. She was cute in her school uniform. Real cute.

"Hey," I said as I walked into the bathroom and looked in the mirror.

I watched her look in all of the other stalls for some tissue and she hadn't found any yet.

"Dis fuck'n school is piss poor. Ain't no paper towel to wipe ya hands and no tissue to wipe ya ass."

The little girl just looked at me and kept looking for tissue until she got to the last stall. She went in and locked the door. I listened to her messing with her pants and then I heard her zipper. I walked closer to her stall and then I listened to her pee. I bent over and looked under the door, she was sitting on the toilet reading whateva was on the wall and I got hot in my stuff. The little girl looked down and saw me looking at her and screamed. She was saying get out, get out. Dummy, I wasn't even in. I tole her to let me see her cat... let me see her pussy. She started screaming. She jumped off the toilet and I saw it. She didn't have no hair on it. She pulled up her pants and was screaming for me to move. I couldn't help but laugh. By now I was laying on the floor and I started grabbing at her legs and she was screaming louder. Then the door opened and another little girl came and walked right back out. I continued to grab at the screaming girls legs telling her to let me see her cat when I heard a man's voice. I looked up and it was Mr. Terry coming in.

"Get off the floor. Get up," he said. He got on his walkie talkie and told somebody he found me and walked all the way in. The little girl in the stall was crying and screaming get out when he asked is somebody in there? He walked over to the door and knocked and said sweetie you can come out.

The little girl started speaking in Spanish and she wouldn't open the door. She said something like no, she trying to get me. I started laughin'. The shit was funny to me.

"Ain't nobody trying to get her lil' ass," I said giggling.

"Then why were you laying on the floor?" asked Mr. Terry.

"Who was laying on the floor?" said Officer Morrison, walking into the bathroom.

"Get out, get out!" said the little Spanish girl still in

the bathroom stall.

"Yes get out, get out!" I said. "This is the girls bathroom and there are to many men in here," I said laughing. "One tall bald head fuck'n po-po and a short ball head fucker. Get out, get out!" I mocked the little Spanish girl.

"Take her outta here Morrison. She's making things worse. I have to get this little girl outta this stall," said Mr. Terry.

"Come on let's go," Officer Morrison said walking closer to me.

"Don't you touch me!" I screamed. "Don't you fuck'n touch me!" I thought of Big Boy. He was tall and big like him. Big Boy was darker, but to me they both had the same scary smile. His hands were big like 'em to. "Don't fuck'n touch me!" I said walking away from him and towards the door.

"Let's not make this difficult. Let's just walk out and go to the office," he said walking toward the door following me, but then he got too close and I swung.

"Whoa, you trying to hit me? Nah, you must be crazy," he said grabbing me by my arm. I was trying to get away when he said, "Now I'ma put the cuffs on ya." He grabbed my other arm and held both of them with one hand. He was strong like Big Boy to. He took out his handcuffs and Mr. Terry was like, "Why you do dat? All you had to do was just go ahead and walk to the office." he said with his eyes all big and shit. Looking like a fish.

But it was to late. Officer Morrison had walked me to the office with my hands behind my back in cuffs.

I heard Mr. Terry still trying to get the little Spanish girl out of the bathroom when I saw Ms. Brown, Mrs. Woodrow, and Ms. Betty coming down the hall. Shit, they called Ms. Betty. She just looked at me and shook her head.

"Why are you doing this?" she asked.

I just stared at her. Ms. Brown looked at me like she felt sorry for me. Mrs. Woodrow just looked.

"Sorry ladies, but she swung on me and I had to restrain her," Officer Morrison said. "I will take her to my office and you can meet me there. We are going to have to write a report because of the young lady in the bathroom. Terry is still trying to get her out. Ms. Brown you might want to get Ms. K. She is speaking English and Spanish and she won't come out of the bathroom stall."

Chapter Fifty-Five

Ms. Brown

As I walked to get Ms. K, all I could think about was the bathroom stall. I remember my bathroom romps. I was in the fourth grade when we had to have bathroom partners. We would go to the bathroom and play in the water and talk. When one day my bathroom partner wanted to play a new game and said it would be fun. I was down with that because she was my friend. She told me to pull my pants down and lay down on the floor on my stomach. I remember thinking this is weird but I did it. She pulled her pants down, too, and laid on top of me. She was pumping my butt and asking me wasn't this fun? I told her yes and then she let me do her. I liked the way her skin felt because it was soft. I did what she did for a little while then I got up and went back to class. For weeks, we would go to the bathroom just to dry hump. That's what this other girl said *it* was. She had told me she was humping with a boy in the back of her father's old car in her backyard. She said sometimes that she would do it with her girl cousin when she stayed the night. The more I did it the more I began to like the feeling. I liked it so much that sometimes I would dry hump with my teddy bears at home until my mother caught me on the bathroom floor. When I think about it now, we always seemed to dry hump in the last stall of the bathroom where the little Spanish girl wouldn't come out of. We would even wait for the last stall if someone was using it. Wonder why I use the last stall now when I go to the bathroom in public places… Do I feel safe or is it just habit? My fear is that it is an old unhealthy habit from my road map of sexual introduction. Hope she doesn't get too messed up over this. For a long time I was and to this day a small part of me still is.

"Hey K," I said walking in to her room while she was on her computer.

"Que pasa mi hermana? What up, Brownie?"

"We got a problem in the A-wing. We found the red–hair, freckled–face girl in the sixth-grade girls' bathroom with a little Spanish girl."

"Oh no! What happened?" she asked getting up from her computer chair and walking towards me.

"We don't know just yet. She won't come out of the bathroom stall. She is speaking both Spanish and English, Morrison said. She is probably scared. Will you come and get her out of there?"

"Of course."

As we walked out of the room all I could think was I wish someone had gotten me out of there, too.

Chapter Fifty-Six

Ms. Wilson

"Who in the world is calling me this time of night?" I looked at the clock and it said 10:26. Calvin looked at me as I picked up my cell phone while we laid in bed watching the news. I didn't recognize the number but answered anyway.

"Hello," I said with a slight attitude in my voice. No one said anything I just heard breathing. "Hellllooooooo." Again, the person was just breathing. "Alright, damn it..."

"Ms. Wilson," said a low sniffling voice.

"Who is this?"

"It's me. You said I could call when I needed to talk and I thought, well, I am sorry for calling so late," he said with a shaky voice.

"Hey sweetie, are you okay?" Calvin sat up and looked at me. I covered the phone and told him who it was. He nodded, got up, and went into the bathroom.

"What's up? You don't sound good. What's going on?"

"Unk hasn't been home since around 5 and I don't know where he's at."

"Oh, did he say where he was going before he left? Maybe he went to a friend's house or something." I didn't believe the words I just said and I know he didn't either. The anger in his uncle's eyes was one that could not and would not be controlled. His own boys had crossed the code of the street. Even I knew that. If his uncle had been gone for 5 hours, God only knows what he has done.

"No. He just told me he'd be back and that was a long time ago. I don't know Ms. Wilson. The dudes he hangs with most of the time are the dudes I told you about today."

"Umm, Okay. Well baby, he found out a lot of information today and he may just need some time to take it all in," she said while getting out of the bed. "I am sure today was just as stressful for him as it was for you." Shit that was an understatement, I thought. I can only imagine how he felt when he found out that his own nephew was being molested by his boy while he was in the house. He is probably blaming himself. He looked so defeated and pissed off, but who could blame him?

"I just hope he hasn't done anything bad, Ms. Wilson. I don't have anyone else. My brother hasn't been around and I wouldn't know where to find 'em and I don't want to go into foster care. He told me he would take care of me," he said sniffling.

My heart was breaking and he was crying. He had probably been crying all day. Here he was on the telephone with me, his teacher; not his mom, brother, aunt, uncle, or any other family member, but his teacher looking for answers. I didn't have any to give. What happens when you have no answers to give? "Well, first of all he is not mad at you. I do think he is upset about what has been happening to you. I know that he will remember that he is all you have and he wouldn't want to jeopardize that."

"He said that he's not going back to jail. He said he's gotta take care of me."

"Then that's what you believe. He is gonna take care of you and he will be home soon. He just needed some time alone to get his thoughts together so he can help you." God I hope.

"You think so Ms. Wilson? You think that he really just needed some air, because when he left here I just knew that he was going to fuck, oops sorry Ms. Wilson, um mess somebody up."

"It's alright, because that word is appropriate for tonight and tonight only." He giggled and that made me feel better. I giggled, too. I needed to laugh because this conversation was too deep for me. I thought staring out my window. "I am sure he wants to get those men that have been… um, have been… um, but we are going to let the police handle this. Like we told you earlier, what they are doing is a crime and they will pay for it." He got quiet. Too quiet.

"Hey, Ms. Wilson, somebody just came in. I gotta go. I will call you tomorrow okay? Bye."

"Is it your uncle?" Dayum, he hung up before I could make sure it was his uncle. I put my phone down then I heard Calvin coming back from the bathroom. He grabbed me around my waist from behind and hugged me.

"Hey, how is he doing?" he asked snuggling his nose in my neck.

"Babeeey, I don't know. The uncle has been gone most of the day and you know he probably went looking for them. I think he just got back in the house. This is gonna get ugly. It may never make it to court."

"Well, for real, what happened is really messed up and a man is gotta be a man and protect his own. He probably feels like he failed as a protector, but best believe he's gonna make it right."

"But honey, if he does something stupid, then who is the boy left with? No one. His uncle is all he has."

"Listen, their life is different from yours. They don't believe in the justice system the way you do and that is why I will always be employed. Street justice is real and that is more important than the judicial system. You should hear them when they are not in lock down. The street never leaves their mind just because they are locked up. For some of them, the streets run in their blood. It's all they know. There is a street code of conduct, if you will. No snitching, no messing with the family, and no messing with the money. He is gonna do what he has to do for his family and if that means revenge then so be it," Calvin said sitting down on the bed.

"But Babe can't you talk to him? You're a correctional officer. Remind him why he doesn't and shouldn't want to go back. Man to man," Willie said wrapping her arms around his shoulders.

"I can't do that, Babe. What do I look telling a man how to handle his family affairs? He lives by the street code," he said shaking his head. He pulled Willie around so she could face him. "I didn't want to say it, but now you're too involved. I know how you feel about this young man and you wanna help, but he has a guardian. Let him take over now. You have done your part. He will get the help that he needs and you can still be there, but just step back some. Okay?" he said kissing my hands.

I kept quiet because I knew he was right. I nodded my head and let it be. His uncle was going to handle this the way he saw fit. I am not his mother, just his teacher and really what more can I do? As a teacher, we have many hats—counselor, adoptive mother, nurse, lunch lady, driver, coach, supporter, and educator. Funny, how during those new teachers' meetings, nobody tells you about the many hats you wear. How touching a child's life goes beyond what you teach them, but how you treat them. And, that today's children have issues that may knock you on your butt. Teaching is almost like motherhood, you're never truly prepared. You don't know what the child will look like, how they will behave, and you learn as you go.

We leave life-long foot prints in a child's journey; I just wish their journeys weren't so damn hard.

CHAPTER FIFTY-SEVEN

Ms. Brown

The next two days at school were very quiet. The kids were calm today and worked without any distractions. Everybody had heard about what happened to the red-hair, freckled-face girl and they even seemed in shock.

Ms. K got the little Spanish-speaking girl out of the bathroom, but she was a wreck. She was shaking like a leaf and crying. Poor thing. K walked her to the office so she could call her mother and speak to her because the mother only spoke in Spanish.

I went straight to my room and packed up my stuff so I could go home. I needed to get the hell out of there. This was one of the reasons I liked teaching. I can go home at 2:45. A teacher reports to work 10 minutes before the students and can leave 10 minutes after they are dismissed. Not to say that a teacher's work is easy or done at the end of the day because it's not. You can at least escape the environment if you need to.

As a teacher, you deal with 150 personalities and attitudes a day. Then there are the parents; some of those uninvolved, in denial, enabling, or just over bearing. Not all my parents are like that. I have some who are active PTA members, attend Parent-Teacher conferences, and expect their children to behave and do their work. These are my awesome parents, the one's every teacher hopes for. Unfortunately, there are just not enough of them.

We need parents from the old school, like my mom and dad. When a teacher called and told you something about your child, the parent believed you. A teacher's word was golden and their opinions was respected and appreciated. Now, teachers are thought of as babysitters with degrees and sometimes we are told that to our faces. And then there are days like today. When you can't protect a child no matter how hard you may try or want to. That little Spanish girl maybe scarred for life. God only knows how she may behave because of this. What might this mean to her when she reaches 15, 20, or even 30? How will she behave around people? Will she ever trust people? Will she be scared to go to the bathroom alone, thinking that someone is trying to get her? What will she think?

I wonder had my past actions scarred someone's child. It's amazing how many girls in my fourth-grade class had known about dry humping with boys and girls. How many of us actually thought that nothing was wrong with what we were doing yet we were scared of getting caught. Our little minds were already messed up by someone who taught us how, showed a porno movie, or pictures from a dirty magazine. Someone had exposed so many of us to sex that we didn't even know it was wrong. We just did it. We had experienced what an orgasm was before knowing what to call it. I know I had. The feeling I got was one that was unexplainable, but with my bathroom partner, very attainable.

The one day she didn't come to school I remember being sad. Who was I gonna dry hump with today? I went to the bathroom with another girl and it wasn't the same. I didn't know her and didn't want to do my bathroom secret with someone new. So I waited. When I got home I went in our bathroom and laid my teddy bears on the floor one on top of the other and tried it that way. It worked, but it didn't feel the same. I missed the soft feeling of her behind. I needed someone and not something.

I did it a couple more times when one day, my mother knocked on the door. I told her I was in there and she came on in anyway. Why not? I am her daughter... She has seen me naked and wiped my butt, so coming into the bathroom to get a towel when your 8-year-old daughter is on the toilet is not awkward. She opened the door and before I could get up she saw me. Pants and panties around my ankles with teddy bears on the floor...

"What are you doing?" she asked confused.

"Nothing," I lied.

"Yes you were. Why are these bears on the floor?" she said, picking them up.

I tried to explain to her what I was doing, but it didn't come out right. Damn it, I was 8. How could I really explain it, when I didn't really know what I was doing? She made me get up and give her my bears. I don't remember the conversation we had, but I do remember the shame. An overwhelming feeling of shame and my bears were gone, too. After that, I stopped for a while, but my urge to get that feeling at the end of humping never left. I wanted that weird, but familiar, feeling again.

During that summer, play time was the highlight of any child's day in the 80's. To have to go in the house was punishment. Let your mother tell you to come inside during a good game of kickball, hide-n-go-seek, red-light-green-light, tag, or jump rope and you would cry. Now days, you can't get a kid outside because of reality TV or the internet.

During that summer, I may have done some scarring of my own. I played religiously with some neighbors' kids. Protocol for every neighborhood was that there was one loud family with dirty kids. They lived with their grandmother who they called Momma Mae. Somebody was an alcoholic. The kids were cursed at when an adult was telling them to *get the fuck in this house before I whop yo ass*, and there was always a fight or argument outside the front of the house that would warrant a police visit. Fortunately, these were the best people to play with sometimes because they never had to go inside. They came out early and stayed outside later than anybody else. Lack of adult supervision, I guess. I would only invite the oldest and the two cleanest over, because even at that age, I had to be selective. You never knew when your cousins were coming over, so you had to make sure you had the right type of playmates. During one of our games, I only had one girl over. She was the one about my age and the cleanest. I think the others had gone somewhere with Momma Mae and she was left behind. Our game of choice was jump rope. A rope was tied to a tree so we could play. Back then, kids were good at improvising. All of a sudden, I was hit with the idea of showing her how to hump. Was it an urge for the weird feeling or did I just want to show her what I had learned? To this day I still don't know. I snuck her in my house and into the bathroom, interesting room of choice or habit, thanks to my bathroom partner. I gave her the same instructions that were given to me in the school's bathroom stall and I dry humped her. When I was done, we pulled our panties and pants back up and I snuck her back outside. I didn't see anything wrong with it, because even she knew what to do.

That summer was one of experimenting. I had dry humped or been dry humped by two other people that summer. I almost learned how to hump on a boy who was younger than me and handicapped. He liked me and wanted to *fuck me* as he had heard his momma say to her boyfriend. When I told him I just wanted to dry hump he said okay, but he took out his penis. I wasn't use to that type of dry humping. He wanted me to put his penis in my mouth and he wanted to dry hump my stuff. I didn't want to do that. That was not what I had learned. I almost performed fellacio on him, but was scared, so I just kissed the head and got grossed out. He was mad, but wanted to dry hump anyway. I couldn't with him. Something inside me snapped and I felt dirty, nasty, and wrong.

Had I scarred them? Were we all already scarred? Was I like the red–hair, freckled–face girl who wanted to get the Spanish girl? I had been taught by a child and had taken advantage of a child while I was a child. Who protected my mind? My parents were always there to take care of me. They loved me and protected me, physically, to the best of their ability. But, we should have talked earlier. Can't blame them. They lived in the south, where black folks didn't discuss things like that. So you can't hold them accountable for talking about something no one talked to them about either. The cycle continued. The abuse in the black community hasn't stopped, just reinvented itself into things much worse. This is why we need to talk to our kids, about everything. This is why I talk to my students about the world and how hard it can be.

If my parents and I had had the conversation about bad touches and sex earlier, would that have saved me? I really don't know, but what most parents think is that their child would not be abused during that time anyway. That was not a plight of the world around the early 80's. Drugs, kidnapping, Reagan, and this new music called hip-hop was what filled the television airways. The issue of bad touches got a plug here and there, but no real attention until 2 to 3 years later. By that time, my classmates and I were going to middle school, leaving our dry humping days behind. We were walking into our paths of promiscuity, boys, finger popping, kissing under the steps, and getting our butts grabbed. Sex had already been introduced the wrong way by cousins, girls, boys, uncles, dirty magazines, and even by reading the first few pages of the Color Purple. We were all scarred in some way. I always wondered if I had scarred them, like I had been scarred by my bathroom partner and my cousin. Lord, please forgive me if I have. I have yet to truly forgive myself.

I turned off my classroom lights and closed the door.

Chapter Fifty-Eight

The Boy

Unk came in the house breathing real hard. Sweat was running down his face and his eyes looked crazy. He looked out the window, locked the door, and sat on the couch. I just stared at him. He looked at me and went in the kitchen. He grabbed a Heineken out of the fridge, drunk half of it, and came back and sat on the couch. I just watched him and then he told me to sit down.

"There are some things that I need to talk to you about and I just need you to listen. Aight?" Unk said looking me dead in my eyes. I nodded yes and sat back deeper into the sofa...

"I want you to understand that I am not mad at you. I am mad at what happened to you and why it happened." Unk took like three long breaths and his leg started to shake like it did when we met with Mrs. Woodrow and Ms. Wilson. I didn't know what he meant by 'why it happened though', and when I was about to ask he started talking again.

"Me and ole boy was up in Jessup together serving the same type of bid with almost the same 'mount of time. We both had possession charges with a gun charge. It was my first and his second. He probably tole you 'bout being up in Jessup, but let me explain to you what happened." I nodded again.

"He was my celly for most of my time and we was cool. We became real tight and we talked about how we was gonna change da game when we got out. But while we was in dere we had to survive." Unk took another breath. "Um, we, um we took care of each other while we was locked up, if you know what I mean?" Unk just looked at me for a while and I guess my face must have told him I didn't understand 'cause he went on. "I was on top. He was on the bottom."

I had heard that before when my brother told me about faggy boys. I thought about it for a minute and then I knew. My eyes got big and my mouth dropped open a little bit. I couldn't believe what Unk just said. He was… with the man with the purple bag?

"Trust, it was for survival. I nevah thought I'd tell anybody, but I didn't expect him to do dat to you. See he was a lil' jealous because I got out before him and I tole him when I left about ya ma being sick, me having to hold it down for y'all, and that I was gonna go legit. I tole 'em we could be cool, but I didn't want to go in to bidness wit 'em. He said dat was cool, but I guess it wasn't. That otha dude you was talkin' 'bout became his celly when I left. I tole 'em to holla at me when he got out. See, when I got out, I came straight to y'all. I had to take care of fam, ya know? So when he got out he thought I was playin' and still wanted me to set up shop with him, but I tole him nah. I had some money saved from before I got locked up, so when I got out I'd be straight 'til I got back on my feet. I was gonna be straight for a minute anyway. 'Sides, my focus was different. Didn't wanna be in da game no mo. I tried stayin' cool with dem, but dat didn't work out. Dats why he stopped coming 'round so much. I had no idea that he would have you coming to 'im. At his crib, no less. Dats why I was so mad when I saw you at his crib dat day when yo lil' ass should'a been at school. I thought he was tryin' to get you to hustle fa him. We had words and den dat was it. What he is doin' to you is fucked up and he is gonna get his yous best believe dat. His two boys already got deres. Know wut I'm sayn'? Dat niggah is next."

"Dayum. So that's why you were gone so long?"

"Yeah, but I had saw ya brovah, too. Tole 'em you needed him real bad and dat he needed to come see you."

My heart was beating so fast I felt it in my throat. "You told 'em?"

"Nah, not yet. He was wit his boys. Dat wasn't da right time to talk. Tole 'em to meet us tomorrow at da park and we can tell 'em then. Besides dat Mrs. Woods lady…"

"Her name is Mrs. Woodrow, Unk."

"Oh my bad," he said laughing. "Mrs. Woodrow wants you to come back early, so you can start your session with that physc dude, Dr. Tibbs."

"I gotta?"

"Yeah man, you gotta. Truth, it may be good to talk to him 'bout dat and 'bout ya ma. So you go back on Wednesday. Dats what Mrs. Harris said... Cool?"

"Aight, cool."

"So we meet ya brovah tomorrow and den we get da shit movin' again. School on Wednesday." Unk looked at the clock, "Yo it's late. Time to go to bed. Everything is cool. I got you, aight?"

"Cool." I went upstairs and could barely sleep. I didn't wanna tell my brother about what was going on, but Unk said I had to. He was like, he is fam and he needed to know and hear it from us and not da streets. We needed each other and either I had to or he would tell him. Either way, he was gonna find out.

The next morning I got up crazy early. Went straight down stairs and got some cereal. Unk wasn't up yet, so I chilled. I looked at the clock and it was like 6:45. I wanted to tell Ms. Wilson what was going on. I wondered if she'd be up this early since I called so late last night. I dialed her number and she picked up on the second ring.

"Good morning," she said.

"Uh, hey Ms. Wilson, it's me."

"I know. I saved your number last night so I wouldn't forget. What are you doing up so early? Was that your uncle who came in last night?"

"Yeah, it was him and that's why I called."

"Is everything alright?"

"Yeah, he's straight." I was going to tell her how he beat up those two guys last night, but decided against it... He got one on Fulton and Harlem in the park, the other on Lafeyette at the liquor store, and that he was looking for the man with the purple bag. I told her that I would be back this week and wanted to know if we could have lunch and I'd tell her then. "Well, today me, Unk, and my brother are gonna hook up."

"Your brother, really?"

"Yeah, Unk found him and we are gonna meet up so we can talk."

"That's wonderful. Good for you. Your mom would be so happy."

"I know. I gotta tell him what's been going on because Unk said I start counseling soon."

"That's awesome. So you guys are meeting today?"

"Yep and guess what? I get to come back to school tomorrow."

"I know. I heard. Great! Can't wait to have you back. You gotta lot of work to do."

"Yeah, I know, but I'm ready."

"Good, me too," she giggled.

"Aight, Ms. Wilson. I'ma let you go."

"Okay, good luck today and call me if you want. I will see you tomorrow."

"Okay, bye Ms. Wilson."

Unk was coming down the stairs and asked, "who dat?"

"Ms. Wilson," putting down the telephone.

"Oh, you tole her about today?"

"Yeah, I talked to her last night, too. I was worried. She was cool. She knew you'd be back for me and she was right."

"Cool. She good peoples."

"Yep, she is."

"Aight, go get dressed. I wanna stop by the mall and get you some gear fa school 'cause it's starting to get warm and then we will meet ya brovah."

We went to Security Mall and got me some jeans, shorts, and shirts. We got some bourbon chicken at the food court and then we were out. Unk was smiling. I hadn't seen him do that in a while. We decided to walk through the basketball court to meet my brother. There was a ball there and Unk picked it up and started dribbling and shot for a three pointer.

He missed and I laughed. I got the rebound when I heard two pops. Unk yelled and grabbed his shoulder and started running towards me. I felt my chest, looked at my hand, and it was red. Unk was yelling for help.

CHAPTER FIFTY-NINE

The Red-hair, Freckled-face Girl

Dear Diary,

I finally told Ms. Betty everything that happened. Like always, I had no choice:

My mother was going to take me to the mall to do my Easter shopping. She was going to da doctors first and then coming back for me. So I got dressed and waited on the couch for her. She was suppose to be back between 3 and 3:30. I waited and waited on that couch for my mother and she never showed.

"Where in the hell is your mother?" he asked with a slur.

"I don't know. She said she would be here by 3 o'clock." When I looked at the clock I couldn't believe my eyes. It said 7:13.

"She betta hurry da hell up. I got shit to do," he said as he sat down next to me on the couch.

I immediately got up and looked out the window to see if she was coming. She wasn't so I sat on the other couch and looked at the TV. I didn't feel comfortable sitting that close to him, touching me. I didn't like him staring at me either.

"Girl your thighs is fat," he said. "Who you been letting touch dem?"

"Ain't nobody been touching on me," I said squirming around.

"Girl quit lying. You know I been checkin' on dat. I know somebody trying to get at you. Been thinkin' bout gettin' wit ya my dayum self."

"Euuh. I wanna get wit you? You're my mother's boyfriend. Dat's nasty."

"Dat ain't nasty. It's natural," he said laughing, holding his stomach and scratching himself.

He rubbed my thigh again, I moved his hand. "You crazy. Get away from me," I said as I got up.

"Come here, ya lil' bitch. Quit playin' games and let me see dat," he said while grabbing my arm.

"I ain't playin'. Let me go," I said trying to get my arm free.

His grip on my arm got tighter and he grabbed my pants with his other hand. I fell on the love seat and he pinned me down. So I began to scream for him to stop it, as loud as I could, 'help me'. I ain't know who I expected to help me 'cause wasn't nobody home but me, him, and my lil' brother and he was sleep. I kept looking at the door hoping my mom would come in and get 'em off me, but she didn't. I started screamin' and kickin' and that's when I really pissed 'em off.

"Shut the fuck up!" he said and slapped me.

I couldn't believe he hit me. I had saw him hit my mom before, but he had nevah hit me. I stopped screamin' and kickin'. I felt dizzy and my face was stinging. He looked down on me and began to unbutton my pants and pulled them down around my ankles. I didn't move. I was to scared to move, so I started to cry.

"Aww, why you crying?" he asked, sounding like he really gave a fuck. I knew he didn't so I didn't say nuttin'.

He pulled up my shirt and began rubbing on my chest really hard. I flinched because it hurt, but he didn't even notice. He was mumbling something about my sweet ass and then he unbuttoned his pants.

I began to cry harder and then he noticed my tears. He said, "oh baby don't cry. I'ma make it betta." He got on his knees and did something I only heard people talk about. I felt his tongue on my stuff. He moved his tongue around and I didn't move. I let him. I didn't cry as hard, but the tears still ran down my face. I don't know, I guess I liked it a little.

"See I tole you I could make you feel betta," he said smiling. "Now come, do me."

"What? I ain't doin' dat."

His smile left and he got angry. "You jus like ya movah. Want somebody to eat her pussy and won't give up no head. Fuck dat." He pushed me back onto the couch and took it out. I began to cry again and I covered my mouth. He was trying to put his thang in my mouth.

"If you bite me you, lil' bitch, imma fuck you up," he said spitting while he talked. I moved my head back and forth with my mouth closed tight. Finally, he got tired of me moving my head and pushed my legs open with his and stuck it in me.

I was hurtin' all over. What was only a few minutes seemed like forever. He got up and some stuff was dripping off of it. My eyes grew real big.

"Oh you straight I ain't cum in ya. I ain't tryna have no mo babies. Bitches is trifflin' when it come to gettin' dat paper." He put it back into his pants and said, "we cool, right? Shit. I ain't do nuttin' you wasn't 'bout to do with one of dem nasty boys at ya school anyway. Even though you was tight at a mug," he said scratching his head.

"Shit, if you did tell ya movah, she wouldn't believe you anyway 'cause I got her sprung of dis dick right here," he said grabbing his thang. "Shit, I'm hungry," he said as he walked into their bedroom.

He went back into the bedroom and closed the door and left me. I was sitting in a wet spot. I didn't know why da seat was wet. Did he spit, did I pee on myself? It was when I pulled up my panties and jeans that I realized my stuff was wet to. Did I get wet from what he did to me? Don't know. Just wanted to clean up. I felt nasty. I got up and went to the bathroom.

When I got in the bathroom, I looked at myself in the mirror and saw the big red hand print on my face. Nothing different that I could see. The red print was the only difference I saw. For some reason, I thought I would look different after what had happened. I was gonna wash my stuff softly 'cause it hurt, but I just put cold water down there. Went in my room and grabbed a clean pair of undies and went back down stairs into the living room to wait for my movah.

I stared at the wet spot on the couch, got up, and turned the pillow over while I replayed what had just happened to me over and over in my mind. Then I jumped when I heard a door open and close. I was hoping it wasn't him coming out of his room. I waited quietly and realized it wasn't him, but my movah.

She came in the house like she was on time and like I hadn't been waitin' for her all day. She tole me sorry for being late and picked up the phone to check the caller I.D. box. Said she ran into a friend, they got da yapping, and then they went and had a few drinks. She talked like I wasn't even there. She wanted to know had I fed my brother yet or did I let 'em sleep all day... did I clean da dishes?... did I do my homework? She nevah even waited for my answer. The phone rang, she picked it up, and started a loud conversation wit whoeva was on the phone. Since she wasn't paying me no 'tention, I went back upstairs to my room.

Chapter Sixty

Ms. Brown

Got a call from Calvin today at lunch telling me today was the day. I sat there pretending to talk to someone else while Willie told us about how her favorite would be back tomorrow. I excused myself and went into the hall way to talk to Calvin. He needed me to get her to the place they met on Morgan's campus a year and a half ago. I told him no problem. We had a quick meeting today and we would meet him there around 5. That was perfect for him because he was just leaving the Tiffany's in D.C. and knew he would have to fight the traffic.

During lunch, I made up a story about needing to go to The Yard, the campus bookstore, to pick up some sweatshirts and that I needed to talk to her about some issues I was having. She was more than happy to ride with me to talk and go to our alma mater's book store. In between lunch, our meeting, and getting her to the car, I managed to call everyone I could think of to meet us on Morgan's campus for this special event and, surprisingly enough, they all showed up.

When we got to The Yard, after 5 of course, the book store was closed, so we decided to walk around the campus and talk about my made-up dilemma. We walked across Morgan's bridge and discussed the school renovating ideas and about college life when we decided to go back because, in actuality, she had dinner reservations with Calvin. Once we crossed the bridge, back over to the residential part of campus, there stood Calvin. Willie still had no idea what was going on. She looked at me and then at him and shook her head. She was even more confused when she saw her two cousins, aunt, and two sorors coming from behind Soper library and encircling her. She screamed. We all screamed and then the tears started. Standing in front of all of us at the place they had reconnected during Morgan's homecoming, Calvin declared his love for Willie, got on one knee, and proposed to *Ms. Wilson* while the clock at Holmes Hall rang 6. It was the happiest day of her life… of all of our lives, for now.

CHAPTER SIXTY-ONE

The Red-hair, Freckled-face Girl

Dear Diary,

I need to tell you 'bout all the shit I been through. I been trippin' and it finally caught up wit me. I guess I been missing my boo so much dat I just lost it. Well its kinda Ms. Browns fault, to. But, I wasn't gonna hurt her. I just wanted to see her cat. I wanted to see it. Shit, she reminded me of my boo when I saw her, so I guess I don't know. I do know dat I got in trouble for it. I swung on him. I swear I thought he was Big Boy for a second tryna make me suck his thang. I didn't mean it. Ms. Betty is so mad at me. When she came up to da school she only talked to Mrs. Woodrow and Ms. Brown. On the way back to the home she didn't talk to me. When we got there she had me come into her office and tole me that all of dis info was being put in my file and dat the judge was gonna have to look at it before my case on dat Thursday. I was fucked. I might as well forget about going home now. She wanted to know what happened 'cause I was doin' so good. I didn't say nuttin' at first and fuck it, I told her. When I left I ran right into my boo. She looked at me for a while and den smiled. I smiled back and she tole me to holla at her lata. I didn't get a chance to 'cause somebody snitched on her and they went in her room and found all da stuff she stole. She was in the time out room. Later that week when I went to court, da judge was blastin' me out and she was mad at my ma, to. My ma didn't even look at me 'cause of da shit she was doin' to my brovah. He had been taken away from her so she could do some anger management classes. They said that after she finished them we could prolly go back home. She said something about counseling to. But for me, I couldn't go back right away. The judge wanted me to try a different situation. She wants me to try foster care for a minute before I go back to my ma. She wants to see if one on one works betta fa me than the home. So here I am writing you from dis ladies house. She seem cool. I got my own room and she can cook her ass off. I will be here for 'bout 30 days, I guess, and den its back to court. I hope my ma get her shit right 'cause I wanna go home. I didn't see my boo no more and when I tried callin', they said she was moved to another home. I don't even know where she was at. Anyway, I guess she aight. I hope to see her again. I think about her when I play wit myself and when I cum I say her name. I hope she feels me. Anyway, I will write in you lata. I gotta go eat. Dat shits weird to sit down and eat at a certain time. I do and we talk sometimes. But most of da time I just sit dere and look at her while she talks. She got some weird looking eyes, like da boy's movah I use to like.

Chapter Sixty-Two

Ms. Wilson

Lord, I did ask you what could happen in 10 days and boy did you show me. I needed to stop crying and get these grades done. Mrs. Woodrow has already given me an extension and I gotta get them done today so she can run them tomorrow. Okay, whose next? All of these are done. I looked at the next one. It had his name. I couldn't go any further. It was his… His report card that I had to fill out. He never got a chance to make up his work. He was coming back to school the next day. If only he had made it to Wednesday. He would have done all of his make-up work and would have gone back to being the student who excelled like he did before his mother got really bad. He died on the basketball court playing with his uncle. Not even 2 months after the death of his mother we were burying her son. The service was held at the same place as his moms. It seemed like the same funeral except he was the one laying in the casket. His brother and uncle took this one harder than the mother's death. She had a chance to live her life and he had just begun his. Instead of sitting in the back with the other teachers, his brother and uncle asked me to sit with the family. I sat in the front row with Calvin by my side holding me up. I wept like a mother who had lost her child. I cried for the future he would not live to experience. This time I didn't hold back, I didn't have to be strong for him because he was gone. Gone. Calvin was strong for me while he cried silent tears for another young black man gone before his time.

The place was packed with more children than adults. In the row in back of me I heard Brownie sniffling. The place was filled with kids from our school hollering and crying about their friend who had been shot on the basketball court where they played. How many more funerals will children have to attend for their friends under the age of 18? He never even made it to the hospital. He died right there in his uncle's arm with his brother running towards them both. I heard that the man who had been getting the "specialty" was their number one suspect. They had been looking for him and had some leads as to where he was. I know the uncle and the brother are looking for him, too. I heard that the uncle had beat up the other two men and told them to let the other one know he was next. Interestingly enough, those two men are now dead.

What are we to do as educators when the street consumes our kids? How do we mend their broken spirits and restore them with hope? To show them that there is life outside of Baltimore that is so much better than what they know. I wanted him to get a chance to experience that and to live to be old enough to experience love and happiness. To live outside and beyond the hood-rich dreams that videos glorify. I just wanted him to be a kid like he was supposed to be, even in this city. He had the right to a childhood and it had been taken away by a bullet and a hustle that earned him a few dollars.

I looked at my engagement ring and smiled. Even in the midst of my hurt there is still peace and happiness. I just didn't expect to go from being the happiest woman on the earth to the saddest teacher in the system. "So that's what can happen in 10 days, huh?" I bubbled in an A for his grade and went to find Calvin.

Chapter Sixty-Three

Ms. Brown

I took the day off to go to the red–hair, freckled–face girl's court date. I didn't have to go, but I wanted to know what was going to happen to her. I felt partly responsible for that bathroom mishap because we had dropped the ball. None of us, not Mrs. Woodrow, Ms. Betty, or I had talked to her about the bathroom arrangement. No wonder the girl was pissed off. No one had talked to the person that this arrangement affected the most. She had every right to flip with all she had been through and considering the information I found out at court.

Not only had she been sexually abused, but she had started a sexual relationship with another girl in the home, but that didn't shock me. The girl she was involved with was no longer there because of her stealing. I guess that explains why she had been stealing from the mall, too. I am convinced she snapped. She was at the point where she didn't believe anyone cared for her but this girl, until she was shunned by her, too. Her momma picked a man over her and the girl started to mess with another girl in the home and we wouldn't let her pee. Great! And she is supposed to behave? How Ms. Betty found out all of this, I still don't know. She had no one.

The judge fussed her mom out and told her she was unfit and told the girl she couldn't go home. The girl started to cry. She said they would try another strategy, a foster home. That maybe the one-on-one attention would do her good along with some counseling. Her mother would receive help, too, for anger management and abuse. Come to find out she had been abusing the little brother, too. As a means of punishment, she would make the children put on wet clothes, beat them, and then put them in a dark room with the air conditioner on. She'd freeze them damn near to death. Crazy bitch took the knobs off and the plug went outside of the room so they couldn't turn it off. She would leave them in there for hours. That is why she hated the time-out room Ms. Betty said because it was dimly lit and a little chilly. I wanted to kick her mom's ass by the time court was over. She still said she didn't know that her boyfriend had sexually abused her daughter even though she screamed it when they took her away. That is why I am a teacher. I want to protect those who aren't being protected. No one child should have to endure such misfortunate experiences.

So they are going to try a foster home, but it's across town. She will be withdrawn from our school on Friday. I hope it's better for her. She deserves a new start even with all of the emotional wounds she has. She deserves time to heal and be loved. The only thing is, foster homes can be tricky. You never know if the parent is in it for the money or to really love a child. Shoot, if I was in the system I would have taken her, but I am not ready for that. The little girl in me needs to heal first.

When I think about my life and the steps I have taken, I can attribute some of my unhealthy practices to my initial introduction to sex. I had known about orgasms before I knew what they were. I had understood what made my body happy before I was truly developed. I had even continued the cycle of abuse as a child without even knowing that I was being abused or being an abuser. I didn't realize that my promiscuous behavior of sleeping with men and their friends had come from being physically abused by more than one person. I mimicked that incident through my own relationships with men. I never understood why I couldn't have a vaginal orgasm with my ex-husband until I realized that my experience with "humping" for clitoral stimulation had been a practice for me since I was 8. My phobia of fellatio had come from the handicapped boy and the story I heard from a male member of my family who received if from a cousin who was my mother's niece. My suicide attempts and low self-esteem came from the hatred I felt for myself because of the things I had done and those things that were done to me… The self love that I lack and try to find in men even in my 30's… The beauty that I still don't see. *I am the children I teach.*

My soul had been shattered just like so many of the children who sit in my classroom year after year with no one to protect them. Our shattered souls are mirrored images of my past and their present experiences. I see it in their eyes.

I teach because I understand what it is like to be picked on for being awkwardly tall for my age, having freckles, not being a fly girl, or for just looking different. I teach to protect them from the world's fury and from those who have cold hearts. I teach to protect them and to tell them about the real world. I teach to tell them that life is just a bunch of chapters, each one with its own ending. I teach because I love them. I teach because they deserve a chance to be children even if it is only in my classroom. I teach for the little girl lost in me. I teach to heal myself.

DISCUSSION QUESTIONS

1. Has *Ms. Brown* changed by the end of the novel?

2. Was it inappropriate for *Ms. Wilson* to give *The Boy* her cell phone number?

3. Does suspension help or hinder students to deal with their emotional issues or adolescent pressures? Did *The Boy's* suspension merely give him more free, unsupervised time to get into trouble within the community?

4. Throughout the book, *Ms. Brown* is concerned about how sex is introduced to our children. How, as a society, have we let this happen? What can parents and educators do to combat this?

5. When working with students how much personal information should a teacher share?

6. Do *The Boy* and *The Red-hair, Freckled-face Girl* seem to be lacking a moral compass or at least lacking the will to resist immoral actions? Who is ultimately responsible for instilling children with morals/character, especially in light of single-parent households, grandparents raising grandchildren, out of control incarceration, and other societal ills?

7. *The Red-hair, Freckled-face Girl's* bathroom usage was poorly formulated. How could her behavior and peer interaction have been better supervised? Should she have been made aware of the particulars of discussion and implementation of visiting the nurse's suite?

8. Was *Ms. Brown* truly jaded against her students or was it just a façade?

9. What have the teachers learned about themselves as a result of their students?